FIRES
OF EDO

ALSO BY SUSAN SPANN

Claws of the Cat

Blade of the Samurai

Flask of the Drunken Master

The Ninja's Daughter

Betrayal at Iga

Trial on Mount Koya

Ghost of the Bamboo Road

FIRES
OF EDO

A HIRO HATTORI NOVEL

SUSAN SPANN

SEVENTH
STREET
BOOKS®

Published 2022 by Seventh Street Books®

Cover image © Paul Schafer, Unsplash
Cover design by Nicole Sommer-Lecht
Cover design © Start Science Fiction

Inquiries should be addressed to
Start Science Fiction
221 River Street, 9th Floor, Hoboke, NJ 07030
Phone: 212-431-5455
www.seventhstreetbooks.com

10 9 8 7 6 5 4 3 2 1

978-1-64506-044-4 (paperback) | 978-1-64506-045-1 (Ebook)

Library of Congress Cataloging-in-Publication Data available on file.

Printed in the United States of America

For every firefighter, everywhere.
Thank you for your bravery and service.

CHAPTER 1

"**F**IRE!"

The cry rang out from atop a nearby tower.

"Fire! Fire!" Other voices echoed the alarm.

On the tower, a bell began to toll.

"Where is it?" Father Mateo craned his neck to search the roofs of the wooden buildings that lined both sides of the narrow street. "Can you see it?"

Master ninja Hattori Hiro searched for any sign of smoke or flames, but the only glow he saw came from the lanterns in the street and the twinkling stars in the evening sky above.

He regretted agreeing to the priest's suggestion that they travel all the way to Edo before stopping for the night.

Had I known the town would be on fire . . .

The Jesuit's aging housekeeper sniffed the air. "Hm. Can't see or smell it, so it's not close. We're in no danger."

"No, Ana-*san*, but other people are." Father Mateo's voice held a reprimand. "We need to—"

Nearby, a man yelled, "Clear the way for the fire brigade!"

Hiro leaped to the side of the street. Ana followed, her movements surprisingly agile for a woman of her age, particularly given the size and shape of the basket in her arms.

Around them, other pedestrians cleared the road and pressed their backs against the wooden buildings. A noodle vendor wedged his cart into the narrow space between two shuttered shops.

Father Mateo remained alone in the center of the street, still looking upward as he searched the roofs for fire.

A deeper voice yelled, "Clear the way!" as a group of men in bulky, padded coats appeared around a nearby corner and approached the priest's position at a run.

At the front of the group, three pairs of men carried bamboo ladders. Just behind them, half a dozen others wielded sturdy staves with metal hooks secured to the upper end. Two enormous, heavily muscled men brought up the rear, bearing enormous woven baskets on their backs.

Father Mateo turned around as if just noticing the pounding of many nearby feet.

His eyes went wide.

The firefighters did not slow.

Hiro leaped back into the street and pushed the priest out of the runners' path. In his haste, he overshot the mark and slammed the Jesuit into the building on the far side of the street.

The fire brigade thundered past. Seconds later, they disappeared around a curve in the road.

Pedestrians emerged from the shadows and continued on their way. Some cast worried looks in the direction the fire brigade had gone; all wore somber expressions, and those who spoke did so in muted tones.

Father Mateo rubbed his forehead.

"I apologize—" Hiro began.

"No." The priest raised a hand in protest. "Thank you. But for you, they would have run me down."

"Hm." Ana grunted in disapproval as she crossed the street to join them. "Everyone knows the fire brigade has the right of way."

"The fire brigade . . . that's how we'll find the fire!" Father Mateo ran off down the street, his traveling bundle bouncing on his back.

"Are you just going to stand there while he runs off into trouble?" Ana glared at Hiro. "Don't you have a job to do?"

I never should have told her about my oath to protect the priest.

Hiro took two steps and paused. "Aren't you coming?"

The housekeeper gave a derisive snort. "Some of us know better than to go running after the fire brigade. Gato and I will wait for you at the *ryokan.*"

"Ryokan Kaeru." Hiro pronounced the name carefully.

"You think I don't remember? I am old, not feebleminded." A well-timed, angry meow came from the basket in Ana's hands. "I'll get our rooms. You keep Father Mateo-*sama* safe."

Hiro opened his mouth to answer, changed his mind, and took off running. Despite the bulky traveling bundle on his back, he caught up with Father Mateo within two blocks—just as the fire came into view.

A one-story shop on the right side of the road was engulfed in flames. Tall, shuttered windows across the front of the building glowed with orange light. Tendrils of fire flicked through the shutter slats like the tongues of angry snakes. More flames licked the eaves and danced along the edge of the tiled roof.

Sparks and cinders rose from the burning building, carried aloft by the rising heat. They swirled in the cold night air. The larger ones fell back to earth, where towel-wielding neighbors chased them down and beat them out.

More neighbors stood on the roofs of nearby houses. Some swung dampened towels at errant sparks, while others scooped buckets of water from rain barrels mounted on the roofs and dumped them on the already dripping tiles.

The members of the fire brigade clustered together in the road. The larger basket-carrier stood before them, shouting orders as he gestured to the flames.

A neighbor hurled a bucket of water onto the burning building from the roof of the shop next door. The liquid hissed, evaporating instantly. It had no impact on the flames.

One of the shutters at the front of the shop collapsed.

Flames surged through the opening.

Father Mateo gestured to the fire brigade. "Why don't they do something?"

"Watch." As Hiro spoke, a group of neighbors dumped buckets of water on the firefighters' padded jackets.

Once all of the bulky coats were soaked and dripping, the members of the fire brigade formed a line directly in front of the burning building. The men who wielded long, hooked poles moved toward the storefront. They sank their hooks into the eaves, beneath the tiled roof. On an order from the basket-carrier, the line of men leaned backward. Their bodies strained with effort as they pulled on the staves.

The building did not budge.

"We need to help." Father Mateo dropped his traveling bundle in the street.

"Stay back." Hiro grabbed the priest's sleeve. "They're going to pull the building down."

"But—"

One of the ladder carriers yelled a warning.

Three of the hook-bearers jumped aside as a line of tiles cascaded off the roof like a ceramic waterfall. The tiles shattered as they struck the ground, sending jagged shards of clay in all directions.

Not far from Hiro and Father Mateo, a short, bald man in a wrinkled blue robe cried out and covered his face with his hands.

A moment later, an explosion blew the remaining shutters off the building.

The firefighters ducked and shouted. Flaming debris showered the street.

The neighbors screamed and ran in all directions.

Heated air struck Hiro's face—not hot enough to burn, but still uncomfortable.

In the wake of the explosion, an enormous hooded figure appeared at the mouth of the narrow alley that separated the burning shop from the shop next door. His padded coat was gray with soot. Thin wisps of steam rose off his shoulders, and he carried a young child in his arms. In the light of the flames, his face looked as red as a demon's.

He sounded like a demon, too, as he roared, "Get the roof down NOW!"

Hiro startled. He recognized the man as the second basket-carrier from the fire brigade, and the voice as one he had long hoped he would never hear again.

"Yes, commander!" The firefighters shouted.

The bald man gave a strangled cry and ran toward the man who held the child.

Once again, the hooks of the fire brigade bit into the beams beneath the curving eaves.

The second basket-bearer bellowed, "PULL!"

The line of men rocked back and forth, straining against the poles.

More tiles clattered to the ground. The roof swayed, but the beams held fast.

"They need our help," Father Mateo said again.

"You have no training." Hiro tightened his grip on the Jesuit's robe. "The best thing you can do is give them room."

The commander of the fire brigade bent down and set the child in front of the man in the blue kimono. Before the other man could speak, the enormous firefighter retrieved a staff from the ground nearby and joined the line of men attempting to pull the building down. He hooked his staff on a beam and shouted, "PULL!"

This time, the roof of the building tilted forward.

The firefighters pulled again.

The overhanging roof collapsed.

A shower of smoke and sparks shot upward. Flaming debris flew across the road.

Towel-bearing neighbors chased the embers down and stomped them out as the fire brigade continued to pull the flaming building down. As the walls collapsed, the firefighters used their staves to push and pull the flaming rubble clear of the neighboring shops and homes.

Father Mateo stopped a passing neighbor. "Do you have an extra cloth? I want to help."

The man stopped short. Wordlessly, he offered the priest his dampened towel.

"I need one also." Hiro dropped his traveling bundle in the road.

The man called out to a nearby woman, who ran forward, carrying two more dripping towels.

Hiro accepted one with a nod and followed Father Mateo toward the fire.

CHAPTER 2

An hour later, the flames and the fire brigade had reduced the shop to a massive heap of burning wood and broken tiles. The shop was totally destroyed, but, fortunately, the blaze would spread no further.

Weary men with blackened faces squatted on the nearby roofs like filthy gargoyles. On the ground, more neighbors carried dripping buckets back and forth from the well at the center of the block. They dumped the water on the flames and returned for more.

With the fire under control, Hiro and Father Mateo surrendered their blackened towels to the man from whom they borrowed them. He accepted the cloths with a deep and grateful bow. "Thank you for helping us tonight. We are in your debt."

Father Mateo wiped his face, leaving a streak of soot along his cheek. "Any honorable man would have done the same."

A deep voice behind them demanded, "Who are you, and what are you doing here?"

The neighbor scurried off like a frightened rat as the commander of the fire brigade walked up to join the priest and Hiro.

The large man pushed his hood back onto his shoulders, revealing a smoke-stained face. "I asked you a question."

The Jesuit bowed. "I am Father Mateo Ávila de Santos, a priest of the Creator God, from Portugal, and this is—"

"You don't need to introduce me," Hiro said. "Daisuke-*san* already knows precisely who I am."

"What are you doing here?" Daisuke demanded. "Were you sent, or did you come of your own accord?"

"If I had come of my own accord, I assure you, you would not have seen me coming," Hiro said. "As for why . . . that answer is for your ears alone."

Daisuke shouted, "Ryuu!"

The other basket-carrier hurried toward them. When he reached an appropriate distance, he stopped and bowed. "How can I help, Daisuke-*sama*?"

"I am leaving you in charge. Stay here until the flames are out, and choose four men to guard the site. No one else gets near the ruins until I return tomorrow morning. Is that clear?"

"Do you think there will be an investigation?" Ryuu seemed surprised.

"I cannot say what the magistrate may do," Daisuke said, "but in the meantime, I don't want the scene disturbed."

"I understand. Would you like the men to bring"—Ryuu looked around as if searching for something—"where is your basket?"

Daisuke gestured toward the fire. "I dropped it on the ground, behind the shop, when I heard the child scream. You may find it there, although I doubt it survived the flames."

"We will look for it." Ryuu shifted his feet. "If not . . . that is, if it's gone . . ."

"I will cover the cost of the replacement," Daisuke acknowledged.

Ryuu bent in an awkward bow. "I apologize—"

"No need." Daisuke waved a dismissive hand. "I know the rules."

Ryuu straightened. "Yes, of course. It's just . . . it hasn't even been two months since you lost the last one . . ."

"And I told you I don't care!" Daisuke snapped. "I will pay for a basket every month, if that's what it takes to do the job correctly. I care about lives and buildings. Ropes and baskets are irrelevant to me!"

"I apologize!" Ryuu threw himself into another, deeper and more awkward bow. As he straightened from this one, he noticed Father Mateo and immediately bowed again. "I apologize for my rudeness. I am Ryuu."

The Jesuit bent forward. "I am Father Mateo Ávila de Santos, a priest of God, from Portugal, and this—"

"You need not bow to Ryuu," Daisuke said. "He is only a commoner."

Father Mateo straightened. "All men are equal in the eyes of God." "Your god is mistaken." Daisuke shifted his attention to Ryuu. "Make sure the building owner meets me here tomorrow morning. No one speaks with him tonight, about the fire or otherwise. Is that clear?"

"It will be done," Ryuu replied.

Daisuke gestured to Father Mateo. "You and your *ronin* servant come with me."

Hiro and Father Mateo retrieved their traveling bundles and followed Daisuke through the darkened, curving streets. The few pedestrians out in the winter night carried handheld lanterns that glowed like giant fireflies in the dark.

Here and there, narrow strips of light spilled from the open doors of sake shops or bled through slatted windows. The combined effect was enough to travel by but, on the whole, the narrow streets were dim.

"Is Edo always so dark at night?" Father Mateo asked.

"This town has a healthy respect for fire." Daisuke's tone did not invite conversation.

Father Mateo slowed his pace until he fell behind the larger man.

When Hiro did the same, the Jesuit murmured in Portuguese, "Does he speak my language?"

Hiro understood immediately. "I think we should be safe to speak this way."

"Is he . . . like you?" the priest asked. "From your clan?"

"He is *not* like me," Hiro replied. "But he is among the people we came to warn."

"His name is on the list?" Father Mateo asked.

Daisuke tilted his head, as if listening, but did not look back.

A few minutes later, the large man stopped in front of a wooden building. A dark blue *noren* emblazoned with the *kanji* for "hot water" hung across the door.

"A bathhouse?" Father Mateo's voice rang with surprise.

An elderly man with hair so white it seemed to glow emerged through the noren and bowed. "Good evening, Daisuke-*sama*. I heard the fire bell. The bath is waiting."

"At this hour?" Father Mateo asked.

The old man straightened. "I proudly offer my humble establishment, at any hour, to the men who water Edo's blossoms."

"Blossoms?" The priest's confusion changed the word into a question.

The old man smiled. "The blooms whose pollen smears your cheek and hands."

The Jesuit looked down at his soot-stained hands as the old man gestured to the doorway. "Please come in. The bath is hot and waiting."

CHAPTER 3

After leaving their sandals and traveling bundles in the bathhouse entry, Hiro and Father Mateo followed Daisuke into the changing area.

The temperature and humidity in the air increased dramatically as they entered the narrow room. A large *hibachi* in the corner radiated welcome heat, while lanterns gave the room a golden glow. Three short, wooden stools straddled a slotted drain in the floor that paralleled the left wall of the room. A bucket of water, a scrubbing brush, and a tiny pot of paste-like konjac soap sat on the floor beside each stool.

A sliding wooden door in the far wall of the room led to the bathing room beyond. Beside that door, a low, square table held a narrow stack of folded towels—an unusual luxury, likely provided as a courtesy to the fire brigade.

Without a word, the men undressed and hung their clothes on hooks beside the entry. They seated themselves on the waiting stools and scrubbed their bodies clean with soap and water.

As he washed the soot from his face and hands, Hiro tried to scrub the unwanted memories from his thoughts as well. He wondered whether he would ever enter a bathhouse without the scent of blood filling his nostrils and a wrenching pain gripping his chest, as if his heart was being rent in two.

Someday, perhaps.

But this was not that day.

Daisuke stood up, retrieved a towel from the stack beside the door, and tied it around his head. He opened the door to the bathing room, releasing a cloud of steam that carried the mingled scents of pine and sulfur.

Through the steam, Hiro could just make out the enormous,

circular wooden tub that filled the room. Clouds of steam rose from the bath, filling the air with haze.

Daisuke crossed the threshold and closed the door behind him.

Hiro finished his own ablutions, knotted a towel around his forehead, and followed the other *shinobi* into the bathing room.

Daisuke sat with his back against the far side of the tub. His eyes were closed.

Due to his size and height, the water reached only halfway up his chest.

Hiro stepped into the tub and knelt with his back to the door—strategically, a weaker position, although that bothered him far less than the unwanted memories the steaming tub and humid room called forth. He reminded himself to stay focused as he settled, kneeling on his heels. Ordinarily, he preferred to sit directly on the bottom of the tub, but on this night he preferred the faster reaction time *seiza* allowed. The position also kept the water below his shoulders, making the difference between his height and Daisuke's less apparent.

It frustrated Hiro to realize he had considered this at all.

He had barely immersed himself in the soothing water when the door rumbled open to admit the priest.

"Does the foreigner know?" Daisuke asked without opening his eyes.

"About *onsen*?" Father Mateo closed the door behind him and entered the tub, lowering himself slowly to adjust to the heat and minimize the disturbance of the water. "I have bathed in them several times, and enjoy them immensely. I understand the mineral content makes the water—"

"He was asking about Iga. About who—and what—we truly are." Hiro looked at Daisuke. "He knows."

The large man opened his eyes. "In that case, enlighten me: what made Hattori Hanzō shackle the famous Hattori Hiro to a foreigner? Men once called you the best in Japan. Has Iga's sharpest blade grown dull with age?"

At one time, the insult might have stung, but after four years in the Jesuit's company, Hiro considered Father Mateo a brother, not a burden. More importantly, Hiro recognized the words as an attempt to goad him into revealing information.

Nice try, but this time I'm not falling for your trap.

"As it happens," Father Mateo said, "I find those words quite rude."

"If the answer to that question is too shameful," Daisuke continued, as if the priest had not spoken, "perhaps you can tell me why you came to Edo? I cannot help but hope Hanzō-*sama* has finally realized he's wasting my talents here."

Hiro sighed. "After all these years, you still lack patience."

At the same time, Father Mateo said, "We bring a message from the Iga *ryu*."

Daisuke laughed. "The great Hattori Hiro, reduced to a messenger? I never thought I would live to see this day. Tell me, Hiro-*kun*, what does Hanzō-*sama* have to say?"

Hiro ignored the insulting use of the diminutive. "Hanzō has reason to believe that Oda Nobunaga has acquired a list of Iga agents, and intends to kill them all."

Daisuke's smile vanished. "And my name is on this list?"

Hiro ignored the question. "Hanzō commands that you return to Iga at once for reassignment."

"Finally . . . but how did Hanzō learn about this list?" When Hiro did not answer, Daisuke said, "As much as I long to leave this backward town, if Oda's agents have infiltrated Edo, we have a duty to find and kill them before we leave."

"Did you fail to comprehend Hanzō's instructions?" Hiro asked.

"I never said I would not go." Daisuke crossed his arms and scowled. "As I told you, I want nothing more. I will leave as soon as I meet with Magistrate Hōjō tomorrow morning and persuade him not to bother with an investigation of the fire. If I disappear tonight, Oda's agents will know we've learned about his list, and the magistrate will raise unwanted questions."

"It would be better to leave in a way that raises no suspicions, if you can," the Jesuit agreed.

Hiro felt a flash of irritation. "We don't know, for certain, whether Oda's spies have arrived in Edo."

"In which case, a little caution will not hurt." Daisuke smiled. "Although I seem to remember caution never was your strongest attribute."

Outwardly, Hiro kept his face a mask. Inside, he seethed.

"It is settled, then," Daisuke said. "I will leave tomorrow morning, after the magistrate makes his ruling about the fire."

"His ruling?" Father Mateo asked.

"On the cause of the fire," Daisuke explained. "By law, any person who starts a fire in Edo—or whose negligence allows one to begin—is put to death."

"You execute people for accidents?" The priest looked horrified.

"For negligence that leads to destruction of property and risk to human life." Daisuke spoke like a father correcting an ignorant child. "It is the law. Tomorrow morning, I will present the facts to the magistrate. The shopkeeper will have a chance to prove how the fire began. If the evidence proves that he was negligent, he will die."

"What if the evidence proves that someone else was responsible for the fire?" Father Mateo asked.

"Daisuke-*sama*!" A shout of alarm came from the outer room.

Hiro and Daisuke sprang to their feet. Father Mateo clutched the side of the wooden tub as the door to the bathing room slid open.

Cold air swirled into the room and dispersed the steam. Ryuu stood in the doorway, breathing hard as if from running. "Daisuke-*sama*?"

Daisuke removed the towel from his head as he left the tub. "Has something happened?"

"We found a body in the fire." Ryuu paused for a breath. "It was a *samurai*."

CHAPTER 4

"Impossible." Daisuke followed Ryuu back into the changing room. "The shopkeeper claimed there was no one else inside."

Hiro followed, with Father Mateo right behind him.

"I saw the body," Ryuu insisted. "I helped the others pull it from the flames."

Daisuke ran the towel over his body. "After more than an hour in the fire, and with the building down . . . how did you see it?"

"I saw the skull when a burning beam collapsed. We rescued what we could, and we found his swords. That's when we realized . . ."

"Did you speak with the shopkeeper?" Daisuke dropped his towel into a nearby basket and reached for his *hakama*.

"Ishii-*san* and the boy had left with Sora-*san* already. You said no one should talk with him tonight, so no one went after them. I came to ask what we should do with the . . . remains."

Hiro finished drying off and began to dress. As he noted the speed with which Father Mateo had also dried and dressed, he felt rising concern about the Jesuit's intentions.

"Have you sent for a priest from Komyō-ji?" Daisuke asked.

"N-no," Ryuu stammered, suddenly uncertain. "I thought . . . y-you are the head of the fire brigade . . . and samurai . . . and I am not—"

Daisuke rounded on Ryuu. "And yet you left the fire scene, *against my orders*, to ask a question that any child—let alone a junior member of the fire brigade—could have been sent to ask on your behalf?"

"I . . ." Ryuu dropped into a sudden bow. "I am sorry, Daisuke-*sama*, I did not think—"

"You did not need to think! You needed to obey!" Daisuke turned his back and put on his trousers, clearly using the moment's pause to regain control. When he finished, he faced Ryuu and continued calmly, "Return to the fire scene. Do not leave again for any reason until I return at dawn. Send someone to Komyō-ji and ask the priests to come and move the body in the morning—but not until after I have the chance to inspect it at the fire scene. Is that clear?"

"Yes, commander. I understand. No one will move the corpse again until you see it."

Daisuke paused, as if thinking. "Has Hiyoshi left the fire site?"

Ryuu shook his head. "He said he plans to stand guard through the night."

"Of course." Daisuke sighed. "Well, at least this time his presence may be useful. Tell him I want him to watch over the remains, and not to allow anyone to see or touch them until I return."

"Yes, commander." Ryuu bowed again. "It will be done. I apologize—"

"Remorse does not excuse incompetence," Daisuke said. "Now go."

Ryuu backed to the door, gave yet another bow, and hurried off.

"Why wait until morning to go back and view the evidence?" Father Mateo asked. "A man is dead. Shouldn't we go tonight?"

"Daylight makes it easier—" Daisuke frowned. "What do you mean, 'we'?"

"Hiro and I will help you investigate," Father Mateo said. "We have experience—"

"Unless you've served on a fire brigade, your *experience* is of no help to me." Daisuke retrieved a clean tunic from a hook beside the door and slipped his arms into the sleeves. "You would only slow me down and, as you know, I need to resolve this quickly."

"Pardon me." The bathhouse owner's voice came through the outer door as it slid open once again.

The old man bowed as he entered the room. "Please forgive the interruption. I have come for Daisuke-*sama*'s clothing." He lifted the quilted jacket from its hook. Gray water dripped from the garment's seams. "My wife will return it to the watchtower when it's clean."

After the old man left and closed the door, Daisuke lowered his voice and said, "I assume you need to warn the rest of 'us' in Edo, also. How can I reach you, should I need to do so?"

"We'll be staying at Ryokan Kaeru," Hiro said.

"I should have guessed." Noting Father Mateo's curious look, Daisuke added, "The proprietor is one of us."

"Does it strike you as strange that Daisuke refused to return to the fire scene tonight?" Father Mateo asked as he walked with Hiro through the darkened streets.

"Not really. As he said, it's hard to see anything useful in the dark."

"He said he wouldn't let us help with the investigation, either." Father Mateo flexed his fingers and rubbed the joints of his scarred left hand.

"And I am glad." Hiro shifted his traveling bundle on his back.

"A man is dead," the Jesuit said.

"His death is not our problem," Hiro countered. "We have more important things to do than waste our time with Daisuke."

The priest was silent for several seconds. "Why do you dislike him so?"

"Me? He was the one behaving rudely."

"The traffic on that road moved both directions," Father Mateo said.

Hiro paused. "Do you remember why I do not fear the dead?"

After a brief pause, Father Mateo answered, "Yes. When you were a child, another boy . . . *Daisuke* is the one who locked you in a storehouse with a corpse?"

Hiro hadn't expected the priest to reach the correct conclusion quite that quickly. "Among other torments, yes."

"Oh."

"His true grudge was against my older brother, Ichiro," Hiro added. "Daisuke couldn't stand the fact that Ichiro was number one at everything, while Daisuke struggled to manage passing marks."

"But since he did not dare to pick a fight with the stronger brother, he decided to take his jealousy out on you." Emotion sharpened Father Mateo's words. "I see."

"But even so," the priest continued in a softer tone, "you must forgive him. Not for his sake, but for yours. You must release the pain you carry in your heart."

Instead of responding, Hiro stopped in front of a two-story wooden building with a black-tiled roof that overhung the street to create a sheltered entry. A small bronze lantern hung from the eaves, illuminating a sign that read "Ryokan Kaeru."

Hiro knocked on the door.

Footsteps approached on the other side. The door swung back to reveal a woman whose unlined face refused to disclose her age. She wore a greenish-gray kimono woven with a pattern of silver lines, and a jet-black *obi* covered in embroidered red camellias. A comb and a pair of silver pins secured her hair atop her head.

"Good evening, Father Mateo-*san* and"—she gave Hiro a curious look—"Matsui-*san*?" She bowed. "I am Kaeru. Welcome to my humble ryokan."

Father Mateo returned the bow. "Good evening, Kaeru-*san*. It is nice to meet you."

"And you also," she replied. "Your room is ready. There is a bathhouse two doors down. It is open late, but it appears you have bathed already. I have prepared a meal, if you wish to eat."

"With apologies," Father Mateo said, "how do you know us?"

"I found your servant waiting at the door when I returned from my evening walk. I do apologize for inconveniencing her with my absence. I had not planned on any guests tonight. She told me about the fire, and that you went to help. Did the fire brigade arrive at the shop in time?"

"Regrettably, no." Father Mateo hesitated. "And we do not wish to inconvenience you. If you have no other guests . . ."

"Guests are never an inconvenience." Kaeru backed away from the entrance. "Please, come inside."

After leaving their shoes on a rack inside the door, Hiro and Father Mateo followed the woman into a cozy common room that smelled of *tatami*, wood smoke, and the tantalizing aromas of grilled vegetables and meat.

Hiro's stomach snarled.

On the right side of the room, a narrow, shadowed passage ran toward the back of the ryokan. Sliding doors at intervals along the passage suggested guest rooms.

At the near end of the passage a flight of stairs, so steep and narrow that they seemed as much a ladder as a staircase, led to the building's upper floor.

"Please follow me." Kaeru started up the stairs.

The second floor of the ryokan was much smaller than the first. A narrow, enclosed wooden passage ran across the front of the building. On the left, a window made of vertical wooden slats overlooked the street—or would have, but for the oiled paper that covered the slats to block the winter chill. Two *shoji* in the wall on the right suggested rooms beyond.

"The second room is yours." The hem of Kaeru's robe made a sweeping sound against the side of the passage as she moved along it. "I gave your servant the ground-floor room at the bottom of the stairs. She offered to help with the household work during your stay, and that room is more convenient, both for her, and for your cat as well. However, I can move her upstairs, next to you, if you prefer."

"That won't be necessary," Father Mateo said. "Thank you for allowing her to help you."

"I certainly won't complain about extra hands, with Natsu gone."

Hiro recognized the name. "Natsu-*san* lives here as well?"

"Do you know my niece?" Kaeru asked. "She is visiting our relatives in the country at the moment."

The innkeeper reached the sliding door at the end of the passage and drew it open.

The guest room had eight tatami on the floor and a decorative alcove in the left-hand wall. Neatly folded quilts and futons rested against the wall across from the door, and a low, wooden table sat at the center of the room, with a pair of flat, round cushions stacked beneath it. In the corner, a brazier glowed, filling the room with warmth and golden light.

The scroll that hung in the *tokonoma* showed a woman standing on a snowy bridge. Her hair flowed freely down her back, and she hid her hands in the folds of her green kimono. Her posture, and the tilt of her head, suggested she was listening to a bird that perched in a nearby tree. The artist had painted her with her back to the viewer, but with her head turned just enough to reveal her face.

Father Mateo entered the room and examined the scroll. "Kaeru-*san*, the woman in this painting looks like you."

She smiled. "I am pleased the likeness holds across the years."

Hiro stared at the scroll in shock. "That is my father's work."

CHAPTER 5

"I wondered whether you would recognize it," Kaeru said. "I recognized you as his son the instant I saw your face. You look precisely as he did when I saw him last."

Hiro indicated a square, red stamp on the lower left side of the image. "I did not know he painted portraits, but I recognize his seal."

"He painted this the year he wed Midori," Kaeru said. "Speaking of which, how is Hiroshi-*san*?"

"Dead," Hiro answered. "Ten years ago."

Her smile disappeared. "Ten years . . . I had not heard."

"Did you know him well when you were younger?" Father Mateo asked.

"Not as well as I would have liked," Kaeru admitted. "But then, we treasure *sakura* precisely because the blossoms do not last. Memories of youthful love are much the same."

She joined them in the room and closed the door.

Hiro moved between the woman and the priest.

"Are you at liberty to reveal what brought you to Edo?" Kaeru asked.

Hiro glanced at the paneled wall. "Is the other room on this level occupied?"

"No. The room beside this one belongs to Natsu-*san*."

"Is she truly your niece?" Hiro asked.

"Merely a convenient tale, to explain her presence—and her frequent absences. The dutiful niece who helps not only her widowed aunt, but other elderly relatives in the countryside. You understand, I could not reveal the truth until I knew your identities with certainty . . ." She glanced at the priest and paused. "*Matsui-san.*"

"He knows the truth," Hiro confirmed. "As for our presence here—we have a message for you, and for Natsu also."

Hiro explained Hanzō's suspicions about Oda Nobunaga's plans to assassinate the Iga agents stationed in Edo. In truth, the list included agents all along the eastern travel roads, but Hiro saw no need to share that information.

"Hanzō-*sama* sent us here to warn you," he concluded, "and sent instructions for Natsu-*san* to return to Iga at once, for reassignment."

"Only Natsu?" Kaeru asked.

"And others, although . . . not you." *In fact, you are the only one on the list he did not recall.*

"This news comes as a great relief," Kaeru said. "I wondered how long it would take for Hanzō-*sama* to act on the information."

"You knew about Lord Oda's list already?" Father Mateo asked.

"Where do you think Hanzō-*sama* got the information?" Kaeru tucked a loose strand of hair behind her ear. "Daimyō Oda's men stay here when they pass through Edo. They believe me sympathetic to their cause—a belief I encouraged, in the hope it might prove useful."

"Does Oda know your true identity?" Hiro asked.

"Of course not," Kaeru's tone grew hard. "Like his men, he thinks me merely a widow who runs an inn with the help of her brother's child—that is, if Oda-*san* knows of me at all."

"And yet, he told you about the list of Iga agents?"

"Of course not," Kaeru said. "Last autumn, a group of Oda's emissaries came to town for a meeting with the *daimyō*. Two of them were spies. That night, as I served their evening meal, I overheard one of them mention a list of Iga agents stationed on the travel road, and an upcoming strike against the Iga ryu.

"I am glad to see that Hanzō-*sama* took my warning seriously." After a pause, she added, "I will ensure that Natsu leaves for Iga as soon as she returns."

"With no offense intended," Hiro said, "I must deliver the message to her personally."

"Of course. You are welcome here as long as you wish to stay." Cold air swirled into the room as Kaeru opened the sliding door.

"Thank you for your hospitality," Father Mateo said.

"Of course." Kaeru bowed. "Now, please excuse me. I will fetch your dinner trays."

"We can eat downstairs—" the priest began.

"Please, wait here." Kaeru closed the door. Her soft footsteps retreated down the hall.

"You just insulted her," Hiro said. "Quality ryokan serve meals in the room."

"I don't like forcing women to carry heavy trays up stairs." Father Mateo set his traveling bundle in the corner and then knelt beside the wooden table.

"Believe me, she does not mind." Hiro knelt across the table from the priest.

"You cannot know that."

"Actually, I do," Hiro replied. "If she cared, she would have given us a room on the lower floor."

Father Mateo changed the subject. "We've found Daisuke, Kaeru, and Natsu. How many people do we have left to warn?"

"Just one: a samurai in the service of the daimyō, who goes by the name 'Yasuari.' He shouldn't be too hard to find. We'll get directions to the barracks in the morning."

That night, Hiro slept more soundly than he had in weeks.

He woke to find Father Mateo already awake and reading the Bible by the light of a single candle. The priest held the leather-bound book in one hand and a candle holder in the other, taking care not to drip wax on the precious pages.

The guest room had no windows, but Hiro's internal clock insisted the sun had risen.

Silently, he rose to a kneeling position and closed his eyes in meditation, but instead of emptying his mind, as Buddhists did, Hiro attuned his senses to the world around him, using his well-trained ears and nose to detect and identify the faintest sounds and smells. He heard Father Mateo's steady breath, the scuttle of mice in the space above the ceiling, and the faint but familiar sound of Ana snoring in her room below. As he inhaled, the faded scents of smoke and incense mingled with the sweeter, grassy odors of tatami and the fragrant tea that had accompanied the meal the night before.

Hiro's stomach rumbled at the memory of the delicious food—the best he had eaten since leaving Iga months ago.

The staircase creaked, as if protesting the weight of ascending feet.

Hiro opened his eyes and looked at the paneled door. "Come in."

Father Mateo startled. "Hiro—you're awake. Is someone here? I didn't hear a—"

Kaeru opened the sliding door. Early morning light streamed through the paper that covered the slatted window in the wall behind her.

The innkeeper carried a laden tray that she balanced skillfully with a single hand. "Good morning, I hope I have not brought your meal too early."

Her gaze fell on the Jesuit's Bible. "Oh, I apologize. I have disturbed your prayers."

"I had just finished." Father Mateo closed the Bible, blew out the candle, and stood up. "Hiro, help me move the futons and the table."

"I can—" Before Kaeru could complete the sentence, Hiro and Father Mateo had stacked the futons in the corner and moved the low, wooden table back into the center of the room.

Kaeru set the tray down carefully. "Would you like more light?"

"If you don't mind leaving the door ajar, there is no need to waste the fuel," Father Mateo said.

"Very well. I will return for the tray, and your servant can clean the room, when you have finished." Kaeru returned to the threshold, bowed, and disappeared down the hall.

Hiro waited far less patiently than usual as Father Mateo bowed his head in silent prayer. His mouth watered at the tantalizing fragrances that rose from the steaming bowls.

The instant the Jesuit said, "Amen," Hiro reached for the kettle and poured two cups of tea.

"Is this *hōjicha*?" Father Mateo sniffed the brew. "It smells like hōjicha."

Hiro closed his eyes and raised his cup to inhale the steam. Despite his hunger, he did not slight this ritual, which he performed as much for pleasure as for safety.

The tea smelled rich and savory, with just a hint of sweetness. He could almost taste it on his tongue.

"Is it safe to drink?" Father Mateo asked.

Hiro opened his eyes and sipped the tea. "It is safe—and it is hōjicha."

"You're sure it's safe?" Father Mateo gave his cup a cautious glance. "I haven't forgotten the last time I was offered tea by the Iga ryu."

Hiro reached for his chopsticks. "That was not the last time you had tea in Iga."

"It would have been, had I tasted it." Father Mateo sipped his tea.

Hiro savored every bite of the meal, from the flaky, roasted fish to the delicate soup with bite-sized cubes of homemade tofu floating in a miso broth. When the soup was gone and the fish reduced to a narrow strip of bones, he started on a heaping bowl of rice. Each chewy grain was cooked to plump perfection.

By the time he finished eating it, his stomach felt equally plump and happy.

Hiro sighed as he set down the empty bowl.

"I agree," Father Mateo said.

Pounding echoed through the ryokan as someone banged on the inn's front door.

Footsteps pattered through the inn.

The banging ceased.

A moment later, Kaeru's voice called up the stairs. "Matsui-*san*? I apologize for the interruption, but you and Father Mateo-*san* have a visitor."

CHAPTER 6

The rising sun backlit the bulky man on the ryokan's front porch, but Hiro recognized him anyway. "Ryuu-*san*?"

The large firefighter bowed. "Good morning Father-*san*, Matsui-*san*. I am sorry for disturbing you so early. Daisuke-*sama* requests your presence at the fire scene, immediately if possible. Again, I am sorry for this inconvenience."

"Has something happened at the fire scene?" Hiro concealed his suspicion behind a neutral tone. "Why does your commander wish to see us?"

"Daisuke-*sama* said that Father Mateo-*sama* offered to help with the investigation. Daisuke-*sama* said . . ." Ryuu frowned and looked up at the eaves, as if struggling to remember the words precisely. "He said, 'Tell them I do not stand a shadow's chance at noon without their help.'"

Hiro silently cursed the code word *shadow*, which indicated a formal request for aid from a fellow member of the Iga ryu—a request Hiro's oath of loyalty did not permit him to refuse.

By contrast, Father Mateo seemed delighted. "We are honored to assist him."

Hiro forced a smile. "Indeed. It's not as if we had something else to do this morning."

"This town feels almost like it belongs in Portugal," Father Mateo said as he and Hiro accompanied Ryuu through the narrow, curving streets. "The buildings are Japanese, of course, but the roads wind much like those in Lisbon."

"Is *Po-ru-to-ga* your home?" Ryuu covered his mouth with his hand. "I am sorry. I should not have asked. Forgive my rudeness."

"Curiosity is not a sin," the Jesuit replied.

"Perhaps not," Hiro murmured in Portuguese, "but a commoner questioning samurai is a crime."

The priest ignored him. "Portugal is the name of my native land. However, for the last few years I have called Kyoto home."

"I have heard about Kyoto." Ryuu smiled wistfully. "They say the streets are broad and flat. That must be nice for the fire brigade."

"I wonder why Edo did not adopt the same design," Father Mateo said.

"We have too many rivers." Ryuu indicated a narrow, arching bridge that spanned a stream a little way ahead. "And the rivers do not run straight. Also, I once heard a samurai say the curves help warriors defend the city, so that must be true as well."

They crossed the bridge, rounded another curve, and the fire scene came into view.

The blackened wreckage lay in a jagged pile, like the remains of a broken, rotted tooth. It filled the air with the acrid stench of char.

Father Mateo indicated the smoke and soot on the walls of the neighboring buildings. "I still find it difficult to believe the fire did not spread."

Ryuu raised his chin with pride. "Edo's fire brigade is the best in Japan."

"I believe it," the Jesuit affirmed.

Four members of the fire brigade stood guard around the wreckage, one at each corner of the now-vacant lot. Their wrinkled, sooty clothes and tired faces showed they had not left the scene since the night before.

A fifth man stood near what had been the entrance to the shop. He stood a full head shorter than the smallest member of the fire brigade, and wore a bright, orange-striped kimono rather than a padded jacket. The hooked *jitte* in his right hand marked him as a low-ranking member of the Edo police. Although he looked as if a decent wind would blow him off his feet, he glared at passersby with a nearsighted squint—the combined effect of which made him appear more comical than threatening.

A lumpy quilt lay on the ground beside him.

The *dōshin* raised his empty hand, palm out, and took a step forward as Hiro and Father Mateo approached with Ryuu. "Stop right there! By order of the fire brigade and the Edo police! Keep moving!"

"Which one is it?" Hiro asked. "Stop, or continue moving?"

The dōshin squinted, wrinkling his nose. "What do you mean?"

"Precisely," Hiro said.

The dōshin squinted harder. "Is that man a foreigner?"

The Jesuit bowed. "I am Father Mateo Ávila de Santos, a priest of the Creator God, from Portugal."

"This is no place for foreigners to gawk." The dōshin waved his jitte. "Move along!"

"I am sorry, Hiyoshi-*san*," Ryuu replied, "but they cannot. Daisuke-*sama* wants their help."

"What does he need them for? I can give him any help he needs." Hiyoshi sounded petulant, like a child on the verge of a tantrum. He waved the jitte toward Father Mateo. "He's not even samurai."

"He holds the rank of samurai," Hiro said.

Hiyoshi leaned toward Hiro. "Who are you? I don't know you."

"Matsui Hiro." He did not bow. "I travel with the foreign priest."

Hiyoshi pursed his lips. "A ronin."

Father Mateo deftly changed the subject. "Have you identified the victim?"

"Not yet, but we will." Hiyoshi gestured to the lumpy quilt, now several steps behind them. "Either his swords will reveal his identity, or someone will report his disappearance."

"They haven't moved him yet?" Father Mateo looked dismayed.

Hiyoshi did not seem concerned. "The priest returned to Komyō-ji at dawn to fetch a cart. They will move him when Daisuke-*san* says they can."

Father Mateo pressed his lips together as if to stop himself from speaking.

"Do you believe the victim was samurai?" Hiro asked.

"The swords prove that he was," Hiyoshi said, "though I can't imagine what a samurai was doing in a bookbinder's shop in the middle of the night."

"May we examine the fire scene more closely?" Father Mateo asked.

"No one does anything until Daisuke-*san* returns," Hiyoshi said.

"Where did he go?" the Jesuit asked.

As he asked the question, Daisuke appeared at the far side of the burned-out lot. He wore heavy winter hakama beneath a padded surcoat, with a set of swords in simple, sturdy scabbards at his waist.

When he reached them, Daisuke traded bows with Hiro and Father Mateo, but ignored Hiyoshi's respectful bow and eager greeting altogether.

Daisuke gave Ryuu an approving look. "Good work fetching the foreigner and the ronin. Where is the bookbinder?"

"Ishii-*san*?" Ryuu asked. "I don't think anyone has seen him since last night."

"Maybe he fled." Hiyoshi sounded hopeful. "If he did, I will chase him down."

"I don't think he ran away," Ryuu replied. "Sora-*san* gave him shelter for the night—"

"I will arrest Sora-*san* also." Hiyoshi raised his jitte. "I will arrest them all. Just say the word—"

"I don't think that will be necessary." Hiro nodded up the street.

A familiar, bald-headed man in a soot-stained kimono headed toward them at a run, with a small boy following on his heels.

CHAPTER 7

The bookbinder slid to a stop in front of Daisuke. He bowed low and remained bent forward, shoulders heaving, as he tried to catch his breath.

The child stopped two steps behind the older man and made a deep, respectful bow.

Hiyoshi thrust his jitte into his obi, clearly disappointed.

"You are late," Daisuke growled.

The shopkeeper straightened. "I deeply apologize. I was delayed."

"You are Ishii, the bookbinder?" Daisuke asked. "You owned this shop?"

The bald man dipped his head in assent. "Yes, sir."

"Do you belong to a guild?" Daisuke did not seem happy to ask the question. "If so, you have the right to request that your guild master be present when I question you."

"I belong to the bookmakers and booksellers' g—"

"There is no such guild in Edo," Hiyoshi interrupted.

Ishii bowed politely to the dōshin. "With respect, while you are correct that our guild has not received the required approval, and thus does not possess official status, we hope the daimyō will—"

"Your aspirations are irrelevant." Hiyoshi pointed his jitte at the bookbinder. "You cannot claim membership in a guild that does not exist. That is a crime! I could arrest you!"

"No one is arresting anyone, until and unless I say so." Daisuke's tone lightened a fraction as he continued, "Ishii-*san*, where is your wife? She should have come along with you for questioning."

"I have no wife. I live alone." Ishii made a backward gesture toward the boy. "That is, with my apprentice. No one else."

"The child I pulled from the fire." Daisuke looked past Ishii. "How old are you, boy?"

"He is almost ten," Ishii replied, "but small for his age."

"And young for an apprentice," Daisuke observed. "What is your name, boy?"

"He is—" Ishii began.

"Are you mute, boy?" Daisuke demanded.

"K-Kintaro," the child stammered.

"Do you always stutter, K-Kintaro?" Daisuke asked.

Kintaro's eyes grew wide. He bit his lower lip.

"You are making him nervous." Father Mateo's tone held a warning edge.

"Have you cause to be nervous, Kintaro?" Daisuke asked. "Perhaps you know how the fire began?"

Kintaro shook his head violently and whispered, "No. No *sir*."

Daisuke shifted his attention to Ishii. "How did your shop catch fire?"

"I do not know," the bookbinder admitted, "but I know that I am not to blame."

"The law says otherwise, if you cannot prove how the fire began."

"I do not know what happened." Ishii looked at the enormous pile of ash and rubble. "This was my home, as well as my workshop. I took not only the required measures to avoid a fire, but others also. I had water barrels in every room, as well as on the roof. I never took an open flame into the shop."

"Where were you when the fire began?" Daisuke asked.

"Asleep. By the time I woke, the flames were everywhere. I could not find Kintaro through the smoke."

"You could not possibly have been asleep," Hiyoshi said suspiciously. "It was barely fully dark when the fire broke out."

"I did not allow open flames in my shop or home." Ishii tried to look at the other men as he spoke, but his gaze returned continually to the rubble. "I always went to sleep at dusk, as soon as it grew too dark to see without a fire."

"You expect us to believe that?" Hiyoshi demanded.

"I ask the questions here." Daisuke gestured toward the lumpy blanket on the ground. "Return to your post."

Hiyoshi looked disappointed, but retreated without protest.

"With respect, Daisuke-*sama*," Ryuu said, "I think Ishii-*san* speaks the truth. The neighbors all confirmed he closed his shop at dusk each night."

Daisuke ignored him. "What did you do when you woke and saw the fire?"

"I . . . I looked for Kintaro-*kun*, of course," Ishii said. "But I could not find him, due to all the smoke."

"How long did you look, before you chose to abandon the child and save yourself?" Daisuke asked.

"I didn't abandon him." Ishii looked at each of the men in turn, as if for support. "I thought . . . that is, I hoped . . . he had escaped, and I would find him in the street."

"Of course you did." Daisuke's tone said otherwise. "What route did you use to leave the building?"

"The door that opened off the living area, behind the shop." As he continued, Ishii drew a diagram in the air with his hands, as if to illustrate his words. "The bookshop occupied the front half of the building, with the living area behind it. Half of the living space had a raised tatami floor. The other half had an earthen floor, with a stove for preparing meals. I kept two water barrels in the shop, one on the tatami where we slept, and two more on the earthen floor, not far from the stove."

His words tumbled out with barely a pause. "I never allowed a fire, or even a lantern, on the tatami platform or inside my shop. The only fire was in the stove, which sat at the center of the floor, far away from any source of fuel. I was not negligent. I swear—"

A high-pitched shriek ripped through the air.

Hiro and Daisuke spun toward the sound.

A woman stood in front of the ruins, beside the lumpy quilt. Hiyoshi stood beside her, holding a pair of blackened blades the approximate length of samurai swords.

The woman buried her face in her hands and wailed.

Daisuke started toward the dōshin. "What do you think you're doing!"

"I did not show her the body." Hiyoshi raised the blades. "Only the swords."

"This is *my fire scene!*" Daisuke thundered.

Ishii watched the exchange, clearly confused.

The woman lowered her hands from her tear-streaked face. Her wailing ceased.

"Forgive me." Daisuke's tone softened a fraction, but not much. "May I ask your honorable name?"

The woman took several quick, shallow breaths and wiped her eyes. "I am Yamada Akiko. Last night, my husband Sanjiro did not come home. I overheard the vegetable-seller's wife saying that a pair of swords was found in a fire. I came to see . . ." She gestured to the blades in Hiyoshi's hands, then raised her own hands toward the sky. "Thank all the *kami*, and the Buddha, these are not my husband's swords."

A tear leaked from her eye and traced a line down her powdered cheek. "Please, do not blame this dōshin. I demanded that he let me see the swords. In fact, I fear I was quite rude."

"Hiyoshi should not have displayed the blades without permission," Daisuke replied. "However, under the circumstances I will overlook his breach of discipline."

"Thank you, noble sir." The woman bowed. "Please excuse me. As my husband is not here, I must look for him elsewhere."

"I pray that you find him quickly, and unharmed," Father Mateo said.

She bowed again and departed, wooden sandals clomping on the packed earth of the road.

Hiyoshi bowed. "I apologize, Daisuke-*sama*. I merely wished to help—"

"I do not tolerate disobedience, especially from *observers*." Daisuke spat the final word out as an insult.

"I apologize, deeply and humbly," Hiyoshi said. "Please forgive me."

Hiro watched the exchange with interest.

Only the lowest-ranking samurai, the ones who had no hope of obtaining any better post, ever joined the police, but even a dōshin technically outranked the commander of the fire brigade, who led a team of commoners. Hiyoshi's groveling made no sense—and yet, he seemed desperate to gain Daisuke's approval.

Once again, Father Mateo intervened. "Speaking of help . . . Daisuke-*san*, you wished to speak with Matsui-*san* and me?"

Daisuke gestured to the quilt on the ground at his feet, but directed his words to Ishii. "Who was this man?"

"What man?" Ishii replied, confused. "What do you mean? Where did you find those swords?"

"I ask the questions here!" Daisuke declared.

"Did any samurai visit your shop yesterday?" Father Mateo asked.

Daisuke shot the priest a look of annoyance, but waited for the answer.

Ishii considered the question. "Five. Two came to pick up finished books. Two others brought me manuscripts for binding, and the last stopped by to inquire about the status of a manuscript in progress."

"What were their names?" Daisuke asked.

"*The Tale of Genji*, chapters nine and twelve—"

"The customers, not the books," Daisuke snapped.

"Oh. That's more difficult." Ishii rubbed a hand across his scalp. "I could probably remember, given time . . ."

"Perhaps this will help." Daisuke snatched away the quilt, revealing the charred remains of a human body. "Who was he?"

CHAPTER 8

Ishii gasped and covered his mouth with his hands. Father Mateo made the sign of the cross.

Only the upper half of the corpse remained intact—and that, only mostly so. The hair and scalp had burned away, exposing the dome of the blackened skull beneath. The corpse's eyes and mouth were closed, the lips pulled back from the teeth in a ghastly grin. The torso had no arms, and the blackened shoulder bones showed through the ruined flesh. The remains of a twisted, blackened leg lay next to the body, barely recognizable as human.

Ryuu had stepped between Kintaro and the corpse when Daisuke drew back the sheet. Now, he put a hand on the boy's thin shoulder and turned the child away from the grisly scene. "Come along, Kintaro. Let's walk to the river and watch the fishermen unload the morning catch."

Daisuke watched as they walked away, but did not object.

Ishii stared mutely at the corpse, shaking his head as if in disbelief.

Father Mateo swallowed hard. "Is it normal for the legs and arms to . . ."

Daisuke finished the sentence for him. "Burn away? Yes. Quite often, actually." He narrowed his eyes at Ishii. "Who was this man? What was his name?"

"I do not know." The bookbinder clasped his hands to his chest. "I swear."

"Your empty oaths do not persuade me." Daisuke jabbed a finger at the corpse. "Explain how this occurred!"

"I cannot," Ishii whispered. "He should not be here." The bookbinder made a helpless gesture. "I locked the shop at sunset, as I always do. There was no one else inside."

"Has it occurred to you that this man—the victim—might have set the fire, and accidentally trapped himself?" Father Mateo asked.

Daisuke made a derisive noise. "Why would a samurai burn a bookshop?"

"Do you remember, last year, a robber disguised himself as a samurai," Hiyoshi offered. "He got away with it for several months. Perhaps this man was wearing a disguise."

Daisuke looked angry, but the nearsighted dōshin continued, unaware. "According to the neighbors, Ishii-*san* is known to work with valuable manuscripts. Perhaps this man intended to rob the shop, and set the fire to hide his crime."

"In which case, he would have left when the fire began," Daisuke said. "Which, clearly, he did not."

He could not have, Hiro thought, *because this man was dead before the fire began.*

"I don't know who he was, or how he got there." Ishii wrung his hands. "A samurai..."

"Tell us what you do know," Father Mateo said. "Every detail you can remember about last night."

The shopkeeper drew a deep breath. "I closed the shop at dusk. I did not light a lantern. I never allowed any flames inside my home or shop."

"Stick to the facts," Daisuke ordered. "Stop trying to make yourself look innocent."

Ishii began again. "After I closed the shop and locked the shutters across the front, Kintaro and I retired to the living area. We ate our evening meal by the light of the oven. Afterward, Kintaro washed the bowls while I banked the fire. After that, we went to sleep.

"I fell asleep at once, as I always do. Some time later, I woke up coughing. The air was filled with orange smoke."

"The smoke was orange?" Father Mateo asked.

"An illusion created by the flames," Daisuke said. "Continue."

"I looked for Kintaro, but I could not find him. My eyes were watering. I could barely see. The hot air burned my lungs when I inhaled. I did look for the boy, but the smoke and heat grew over-whelming. I forced myself to leave, but I truly thought Kintaro had escaped."

"You believe the boy would have left you behind in a burning building?" Daisuke asked.

The question hung in the air long enough to make Hiro suspect Ishii did believe it.

"At the time, I did not stop to think it through." The bookbinder replied. "The flames. The heat. You cannot understand—"

"On the contrary," Daisuke replied. "I understand all too well. Do not forget, I went inside to save the boy."

"I cannot understand how you heard him scream, when I did not." Ishii hung his head. "I feel ashamed."

"You should," Daisuke said.

"What matters is that the boy is safe," Father Mateo said.

"Why did the shop explode?" Daisuke asked. "What materials did you store inside?"

"The glue I use to bind the books and covers can explode if exposed to flame—another reason I did not allow any fire inside my shop."

Hiyoshi bent low, squinting at the corpse. "Did anyone notice that his mouth is closed?"

Hiro had—and had wondered whether anyone else would it point out.

"Does that mean something?" Father Mateo asked.

Hiyoshi straightened. "The faces of people who die in fires do not look peaceful. They die screaming."

"Are you suggesting that this man was dead before the fire began?" the Jesuit asked.

Ishii's eyes lit up with hope. "If so, that proves his death is not my fault."

"It proves nothing of the sort," Daisuke said. "You owned the shop. By law you are responsible, not only for the fire but also all resulting damages and deaths, unless you have persuasive evidence that proves your innocence beyond all doubt."

"That is not justice," Father Mateo objected.

"The law is clear," Daisuke said.

"Someone must bear the blame," Hiyoshi added.

"Blame him." Father Mateo gestured to the corpse. "You have as much evidence of his guilt as you do against Ishii-*san*."

"Arrest the bookbinder," Daisuke told Hiyoshi, "and take him to Magistrate Hōjō. I will gather the evidence I need and meet you there."

"No." Father Mateo stepped between the dōshin and the artisan. "I will not stand here while you blame this man for a crime you cannot prove he committed."

"Then do not stand here." Daisuke looked at Hiro. "Take the foreigner and go. I have changed my mind. I no longer require your aid."

Father Mateo crossed his arms. "We—"

"—acknowledge your authority to decide what happens here." Hiro switched to Portuguese. "We need to leave. Right now."

"But—"

"Immediately," Hiro said. "The situation is not what it seems."

CHAPTER 9

As Hiro led Father Mateo back through the crowded, winding streets toward the ryokan, his thoughts returned to their mission in Edo. He considered asking Kaeru if she knew Yasuari. Generally speaking, Hanzō disapproved of agents sharing information, especially when doing so might endanger other members of the ryu. That said, anyone whose name appeared on Oda's list was in danger already, and Hiro was eager to leave the town as soon as possible.

Father Mateo stopped walking. "All right. I did as you asked. Now tell me: why did you insist we had to leave?"

"Impressive," Hiro told the priest. "You held that question back for almost four minutes."

"This is not the time for jokes." Father Mateo waved a hand in the direction they had come. "An innocent man is about to die, and we could have helped him."

"You don't know—"

Behind the priest, a male voice shouted in alarm.

Hiro grabbed the Jesuit's sleeve and pulled him aside as a heavy pushcart rumbled by. Clouds of steam rose from an opening in the cart's peaked roof, filling the air with the savory scents of pork and onions. Hiro's mouth began to water, despite his recent, filling breakfast.

The man who pulled the cart bowed his head in apology as he passed. "I am sorry! I am sorry! I could not stop in time!"

"I understand," Father Mateo called after him. "I am sorry we blocked your way!"

"For the ten-thousandth time," Hiro said, "men of samurai rank do not apologize to commoners."

"Rank is irrelevant when apologies are due." Father Mateo sighed. "I need to remember not to stop in the middle of the road."

A steady stream of pedestrians flowed past. The men wore padded jackets and robes over thick pleated trousers. Many carried heavy burdens or pulled the handles of wheeled carts. Here and there a samurai swaggered through the street, unburdened except for the swords thrust through his obi. Women in colorful kimono and tall wooden *geta* wove through the crowds, enjoying the winter morning. Most carried parasols to shield them from the sun that shone in the bright blue, cloudless sky.

Groups of porters filed along the road in both directions, walking single file beneath their burdens. A short, fuzzy horse pulled a wooden cart piled high with sacks of rice.

Father Mateo watched the traffic pass. "Edo feels so much more crowded than Kyoto, even though it's just a fraction of the size."

Hiro gestured to the buildings. "Narrow streets."

"Father Vilela thinks this town has great potential. He plans to establish a church here soon. At one time, I hoped . . ." Father Mateo shook his head as if to clear the thought. "Back to the point. Why did you insist we leave, instead of helping Ishii-*san*?"

"Daisuke used a code to request our presence. Between that and his sudden change of heart about our help, I believe he has discovered a connection between the fire and the Iga ryu—but could not mention what he knows with others present. He has realized, as I did, that the samurai was dead before the fire began. And, for the record, I don't think the dead man's legs and arms burned off."

"You think he was dismembered?"

Hiro nodded. "I think Daisuke does too."

"Why didn't he say so?"

"I believe he has evidence suggesting that the victim, or the killer, was shinobi."

"Which means Ishii may be shinobi too," Father Mateo said.

"Not necessarily," Hiro replied. "It is a logical deduction, but we cannot make assumptions, one way or the other."

The Jesuit looked back up the street. "We need to learn the truth before the magistrate executes Ishii."

"If he killed a member of my clan, he deserves to die," Hiro said.

"If he did not, he deserves to live," Father Mateo countered. "I think Hanzō will want to know the truth."

"Invoking my cousin is not the best way to obtain my cooperation."

Before Hiro could continue, a high-pitched voice called, "Foreign Sir!"

Ishii's apprentice ran toward them, weaving deftly through the people and carts that filled the crowded street.

Hiro felt an odd combination of foreboding and relief. He could think of only one reason why Kintaro would chase them down. If it proved correct, the boy would offer a perfect cover story—and excuse—to investigate the fire.

While Hiro loathed the idea of spending any more time with Daisuke, Father Mateo had made a valid point. Hanzō would want to know the truth about the body in the fire, and any connection between the victim and the Iga ryu.

Kintaro slid to a stop in front of Father Mateo and bent forward in a bow. He straightened, arms held stiffly at his sides. "Please, noble sirs." He looked from Father Mateo to Hiro and back again. "My master needs your help. They arrested him, and took him to Magistrate Hōjō. They say my master killed a man and set the shop on fire to hide the body. But Master Ishii did not do that. Please. They will kill him if you do not help."

"Did someone send you to request our assistance?" Hiro asked.

"No." Kintaro hung his head as if ashamed. "I thought . . . I hoped . . ." He looked up just as an enormous tear dripped from his eye, ran down his face, and spattered on the ground. "There is no one else to ask." He raised a hand and wiped his cheek. "If they hang him, I have nowhere else to go."

"Where are your parents?" Father Mateo asked.

Kintaro sniffed and looked at the ground. "Dead, noble sir."

Father Mateo switched to Portuguese. "We have to help him."

"There is nothing we can do," Hiro replied in the Jesuit's language.

"We would need conclusive proof of innocence, which, as you know, we do not possess."

Father Mateo nodded toward Kintaro. "I did not speak only of the trial."

Hiro stifled a sigh as he shifted his gaze to the boy and his words to Japanese. "Very well. Take us to the magistrate."

Kintaro's mouth dropped open. "Truly?"

"Do not make me repeat myself," Hiro warned, "or I might change my mind."

"Thank you. Thank you." The child bowed. "It isn't far. Please, come this way."

"What changed your mind?" Father Mateo asked in Portuguese as they followed Kintaro down the street.

"As you said, I have a duty to learn the truth about the body in the fire," Hiro answered, also in Portuguese. "Our presence in this town defies the orders we were given. Solving this mystery is the best way to avoid—or at least to mitigate—any serious repercussions."

"Then this is not about the boy." Father Mateo sounded disappointed. "I don't want to give the child false hope."

"Any hope is better than none," Hiro said, "and I am not averse to helping the child, if we can. However, you know I will not risk my life, or yours, to help a stranger. Not even an orphaned boy."

Father Mateo said no more, but the set of the Jesuit's jaw suggested his silence did not constitute assent.

CHAPTER 10

By the time Kintaro led Hiro and Father Mateo to the open yard where the magistrate held court, Ishii's trial had begun.

The bookbinder knelt in a pit of sand directly in front of the magistrate's wooden dais, with his hands bound tightly behind his back. Daisuke stood to the right of the *shirazu* in which the prisoner knelt. Ryuu and another member of the fire brigade stood at attention just behind their commander, while Hiyoshi had the dubious honor of standing directly behind Ishii—though outside the pit of sand—holding the loose end of the knotted rope that bound the prisoner's hands.

On the far side of the shirazu, the magistrate knelt on an elevated wooden dais. He was unusually young, and his face wore an alert, intelligent expression that, combined with the long black robes that surrounded him like a pair of wings, put Hiro in mind of an enormous crow.

Heavily armored samurai stood guard on either side of the magistrate's dais. Their breastplates bore the insignia of the daimyō. At their sides, expensive lacquered scabbards gleamed in the winter sun. The man on the left of the dais held a pole displaying a six-foot standard emblazoned with the daimyō's crest, while the one on the right wielded a *naginata* half again as long as he was tall.

The guards stood motionless, like statues carved from stone, but their eyes tracked every movement in the yard.

To the left of the shirazu, a cluster of onlookers watched the proceedings from a polite but respectful distance. To the right, an orderly queue of people—some, clearly merchants seeking resolution of disputes, while others were prisoners bound with knotted ropes—waited their turns before the magistrate.

Kintaro slowed his pace and glanced at Hiro and Father Mateo, as if hoping one of them would take the lead.

Hiro obliged, lengthening his stride to pass the boy and continuing forward until he reached an open space a respectful distance behind the pit of sand.

"Have you proof of the victim's identity?" the magistrate asked.

"Only that he was samurai," Daisuke said. "We found his weapons in the fire."

Ryuu raised the blackened swords.

"You found them personally?" Magistrate Hōjō asked.

The firefighter next to Ryuu bowed. "I found them, Honorable Magistrate. I saw them underneath a burning beam, while I was looking for the other leg."

"The . . . other leg?" Magistrate Hōjō shifted his gaze to Daisuke. "Do legs normally . . . come off . . . in a fire?"

"See?" Father Mateo whispered in Portuguese. "It was not a foolish question after all."

"I never said it was," Hiro muttered back.

"Sometimes," Daisuke replied, with a glare at his subordinate. "Although we try not to discuss such things in public."

"Do the swords bear the owner's name or family crest?" Magistrate Hōjō asked.

"They do not appear to," Daisuke answered. "As you can see, the flames consumed the scabbards and the wrapping on the hilts. The guards, and the blades themselves, are unadorned."

"The blades should bear a maker's mark, if nothing more." The magistrate leaned forward, as if for a better look at the blackened blades.

"The mark is illegible," Daisuke said.

"Perhaps the head of the swordsmiths' guild could decipher it," the magistrate suggested.

"He was the one who pronounced the mark unreadable," Daisuke replied. "His records extend only to the members of his guild, and although he has a ledger that contains the marks of many famous swordsmiths, he confirmed that he had never seen this mark, or anything close enough to raise a question.

"He could confirm only that the swords are a matched *katana* and *wakizashi*, of the type customarily carried by samurai, and asked me to convey his deep and sincere apology for his failure to identify them further."

Magistrate Hōjō studied Ishii. "If the swords were made by an unknown smith, the victim must have been a stranger, newly arrived in Edo or passing through. The kind of person who might be perceived as an easy target, because his death could easily go unnoticed."

Ishii looked at the sand in front of him and did not speak.

"Forgive my intrusion," Hiyoshi said, "but there is another possibility."

Daisuke gave the dōshin a hostile look.

Magistrate Hōjō seemed intrigued. "Please, share your theory."

Hiyoshi squinted at the magistrate. "After the shogun died last year, Daimyō Hōjō spread the word that he wanted to increase the size of his army. Many samurai came to Edo in answer to that call.

"Perhaps the victim came from another province, bearing swords forged by a smith whose style is not well known. In that case, Edo's swordsmiths would not recognize the mark."

"A valid point," Magistrate Hōjō said.

"However," Hiyoshi continued, "the identity of the victim, and even the fact that he may have died before the fire began, does not change the fact that this man is responsible." He gestured to Ishii. "A samurai died, his body burned, and this man's negligence allowed the fire to occur."

Magistrate Hōjō rubbed his chin thoughtfully. "You believe the victim died before the fire? I am disinclined to convict a man of wrongful death—to say nothing of murder—without conclusive evidence of guilt."

Father Mateo exhaled audibly and with relief.

"However"—Magistrate Hōjō raised his chin and his voice, as if to ensure that everyone in the yard would hear—"on the subject of the fire itself, the law and the facts are clear. Fires begin in one of three ways: by natural causes, by negligence, and by criminal intent.

"Last night, the sky was clear. There was no wind. There were no earthquakes and no lightning storms. Therefore, this fire did not occur through natural causes, but by human agency.

"No one has offered evidence to prove what happened in the shop or how the fire began. The accused claims innocence, but can present no proof to support his claim. Therefore, I must rule this a fire of unknown human origin.

"By law, when a fire occurs in Edo and its origin cannot be proven, the person in possession and control of the building where the fire began is deemed to be negligent, and responsible for the fire."

After a pause, the magistrate added, "By law, the penalty for such negligence is death."

Ishii's shoulders drooped.

Father Mateo started toward the magistrate. "One moment, please."

Hiro hurried after the priest with a silent curse.

"Who are you?" Magistrate Hōjō asked as Father Mateo stopped beside Hiyoshi, at the edge of the shirazu.

The Jesuit bowed. "I am Father Mateo Ávila de Santos, a priest of the Creator God, from Portugal. With respect, as you said yourself, you cannot execute this man without conclusive evidence of guilt."

"That is not precisely what I said," the magistrate replied. "And although, in most cases, I would agree with you completely, the law is different—and quite clear—in the case of fire."

"Then the law is wrong." Father Mateo clasped his hands for emphasis. "I implore you. Do not follow it."

Magistrate Hōjō gestured to Ishii. "Why do you care what happens to this man? Is he a convert to your foreign faith?"

"No!" Ishii's head snapped up. "I never saw this man before last night, and never spoke with him until this morning."

"In that case, why does he care so much about your fate?"

CHAPTER 11

"God and my faith require me to care about all men," Father Mateo said, "and to help as many as I can, whether or not I know them well."

"But this man you do not know, and cannot help." Magistrate Hōjō rested his hands on his thighs. "The law is unambiguous. When a fire occurs, the responsible parties must be punished, both for purposes of justice and to deter future fires."

"I respect your wisdom, and share your commitment to justice," Father Mateo said, "but punishing this man would merely stop a tiger at the front gate while a wolf slips in the back one."

Magistrate Hōjō stared at the Jesuit, clearly puzzled.

"That was not an appropriate proverb for this moment," Hiro muttered in Portuguese.

"No?" Father Mateo whispered through a frozen smile.

"In essence, you just told the magistrate he cannot trust anyone." Hiro stepped forward, bowed, and raised his voice to a normal level as he switched to Japanese. "Honorable Magistrate, please forgive my master. As you see, he struggles with our language."

The magistrate looked from Hiro to Father Mateo. "Yes, I noticed."

"Honorable Magistrate, may I speak?" Ishii asked.

"You may." The magistrate regarded him expectantly.

"Two other fires have occurred not far from my shop—that is, from the place where my shop once stood—in recent weeks."

"Do you think me ignorant of that fact?" Magistrate Hōjō asked.

"No, of course not." Ishii dipped his head in a humble bow. "I merely meant . . . the men who make and sell books in Edo are not known for negligence. Our . . . group . . . takes extra precautions against fire. And yet, all three of the recent fires destroyed shops that belonged to men who engage in making books."

"Speak plainly," Magistrate Hōjō said. "Do you mean to imply that someone wants to harm your association? If so, do you have any evidence to support your theory?"

"This is nonsense," Daisuke intervened. "The groundless theory of a desperate man."

"Please—at least consider the possibility," Ishii begged. "Three fires in book-related shops within two months—"

Hiyoshi cut him off. "This time last year, the fire brigade put out five fires in a single month. Edo always has more fires in winter months."

"More importantly," Daisuke put in, "we investigated both of the other recent fires, and ruled them accidental."

"The first resulted from an artisan smoking poppy tears in the company of a prostitute," Hiyoshi said. "And killed them both."

Hiro heard Kintaro's soft but sharp intake of breath, and noticed the child stiffen. He glanced down and saw the boy staring straight ahead, his body rigid.

Hiyoshi continued, "Last week's fire occurred because the owner of the shop could not be bothered to clear away the piles of dust and shavings that accumulated when he carved the woodblocks for his prints. All the neighbors said they had expected, and feared, such a fire for quite some time."

"You do not need to remind me of the facts," Magistrate Hōjō said. "I remember the cases well. As I recall, the fire brigade did look for potential connections between the fires." He looked at Daisuke.

"We did, and we found nothing," Daisuke confirmed. "Nothing meaningful, anyway."

Magistrate Hōjō asked Ishii, "Have you evidence to support your suggestion that the fires had a common cause?"

The bookbinder answered slowly and carefully. "Nothing specific . . . however, a dead samurai could not have appeared in my shop by chance, and I swear by all the kami that he was not there when I went to sleep last night. I did not kill him. I do not know who did. That alone suggests there must be more to this fire than an accident, or even negligence.

"Moreover, had Kintaro and I not escaped the fire, no one would have questioned the number of bodies in the wreckage, had any bodies even been recovered. If the fire brigade had arrived a few minutes later, the flames might have consumed the evidence entirely."

"Two minutes ago, you suggested someone set the fire to harm your guild, and now you claim it was set to hide a body?" Daisuke raised his hands in a pleading gesture. "Honorable Magistrate, how long will you allow this to continue?"

"I do not deny my desire to avoid execution," Ishii said. "But I know, without question, that I did not start or allow the fire that burned my shop last night. I did not kill a samurai. I beg you, please, investigate."

Silence settled over the yard as the magistrate considered this appeal. Even the bystanders waited mutely, as if a single word might tip the balance.

Seconds passed.

After a highly unusual length of time, Magistrate Hōjō said, "I face an unusual dilemma. With regard to the fire, at least, the law is clear. In the absence of other evidence, I must rule Ishii-*san* negligent, and, for that negligence, he must die. However, if I order his execution now, we may never learn the identity of the samurai who died in last night's fire . . . or before the fire, as the case may be. Moreover, if Ishii-*san* speaks the truth, that course of events would allow whoever killed the samurai to escape all punishment—an outcome I find unsatisfactory on many levels."

Hiro could hardly believe his ears. In his experience, magistrates cared more for punishment than justice. Such compassion from the dais was a rare event, indeed.

"Daisuke-*san*," the magistrate continued, "I wish for you to investigate the death of this unknown samurai. Reveal his identity and, if possible, what killed him. As you do, remain alert for any potential connections to the other recent fires.

"To be clear, I do not believe you erred in determining the previous fires were unrelated. I merely wish to ensure no relevant evidence is ignored or overlooked."

"Thank you, Magistrate Hōjō," Daisuke replied. "However, with respect, I must point out that finding any new evidence about the prior fires may prove impossible. No one survived the fire at the calligrapher's shop, and the woodblock carver was executed the morning after his shop burned down. Workers have already cleared the rubble from both lots . . ."

"Surely the site of last night's fire remains intact," the magistrate said.

"If that word can be used to describe a pile of ashes and broken beams." Daisuke gestured to the blackened swords in Ryuu's hands. "The only evidence we recovered bears no useful marks. I suppose I could speak with the commander of the daimyō's guard, to see if any of his men is missing."

"You have not pursued that lead already?" Magistrate Hōjō asked.

"As you know, I am the only man of samurai rank on the fire brigade," Daisuke said, "and I have had no time to go in person. In fact, it will be difficult for me to conduct the investigation at all, because I lack the time to—"

"If the magistrate and the fire commander will pardon my interruption," Hiyoshi said, "perhaps I could be of service in this matter."

CHAPTER 12

"Y ou?" Daisuke's voice rang with disbelief.

Hiyoshi wore the eager expression of a puppy seeking praise. "I would consider it an honor to use my skills in the service of the fire brigade and the honorable magistrate. I give you my word, I will find out the truth."

"You couldn't find your shadow on a sunny morning," Daisuke retorted.

"I have experience with investigations," Hiyoshi told the magistrate. "I understand fires, and how they start. I petitioned to join the fire brigade three times."

"And I refused all three petitions," Daisuke added.

"Why do you want to join the fire brigade?" Magistrate Hōjō asked. "Except for the commander, it's composed entirely of commoners."

"I wondered the same thing myself," Daisuke said.

"You never said so," Hiyoshi objected. "You said I was too blind to carry a ladder and too weak to work the fire hooks. But I never asked to carry ladders. I applied to serve as your assistant, and to help you investigate the fires."

He addressed the magistrate. "I am *not* blind! Please—give me the opportunity to prove my worth."

"You have experience with investigations?" Magistrate Hōjō asked.

Hiyoshi's face lit up with hope. "I do. I assisted Yoriki Sato—"

"Assisted?" Magistrate Hōjō echoed. "The *yoriki* did not place you in charge?"

"No," Hiyoshi admitted, "but—"

"And just how many investigations have you helped him with?" Daisuke's tone implied he knew the answer.

"Two." Hiyoshi paused. "That is, almost two."

"*Almost* two." Daisuke gave the magistrate a pointed look.

"Are you certain you cannot lead this investigation, Daisuke-*san*?" Magistrate Hōjō asked.

"I cannot, but . . . perhaps I may suggest a more appropriate alternative." Daisuke gestured to Father Mateo. "You could appoint the foreign priest to conduct the investigation. I would, of course, provide any assistance he requires."

"The foreign priest?" Hiyoshi and the magistrate exclaimed in unison.

Hiro barely managed to conceal his own surprise. However, as the moment passed, he suspected he knew the reason for the other shinobi's change of heart: *he doubtless thinks that Father Mateo will agree to conceal any inconvenient truths.*

Although the Jesuit seemed startled too, he recovered quickly. "It would be an honor to assist you. Matsui-*san* and I have investigated numerous murderers, and succeeded in finding the killer every time. We will do our best to reveal the truth about this fire also."

"These men are strangers," Hiyoshi protested. "They know nothing of Edo, or the law—"

"Which merely means they have no preconceptions to distract them from the truth," Daisuke said. "As to the law, I will gladly provide any relevant information."

"They have no authority, and no official rank," Hiyoshi persisted. "Matsui-*san* is ronin!"

"But still samurai," Daisuke said, "and I understand the foreign priest carries noble rank as well. They require no more."

Hiyoshi gestured to Father Mateo. "We do not know this man's true history, or his motivation. We know only that he serves a foreign god."

"I assure you, my only motivation is to help," Father Mateo said, "and God, like me, desires only truth."

"Enough." The magistrate raised a hand to stop the argument. "I have made a decision. Father Mateo-*san* and Matsui-*san* will investigate the regrettable death of the unknown samurai, in the hope of discovering his identity and confirming the causes of the recent fires. Daisuke-*san*, Hiyoshi-*san*, you will both provide these men with any assistance they request. I will send word to Yoriki Sato, instructing him to release Hiyoshi-*san* from all other duties for the duration of the investigation."

Daisuke bowed. "As you command, Honorable Magistrate."

Hiyoshi crossed his arms and set his jaw.

The magistrate continued, "I will suspend my verdict in this matter, and reconvene the trial of Ishii the bookbinder in one week's time."

"What will happen to Ishii-*san* during the investigation?" Father Mateo asked.

"We will lock him in the jail," Hiyoshi said, "to ensure he does not escape."

The Jesuit addressed Magistrate Hōjō. "With respect, I request that you leave him free. I may need his help with the investigation."

"He told us he knows nothing about the fire, or the samurai," Hiyoshi said. "If we don't lock him up, he will run away."

"Or cause another fire," Daisuke added. "On this point, I agree with Hiyoshi-*san*."

"I will not flee or start a fire," Ishii put in. "I swear it on my life."

"I cannot allow it," Magistrate Hōjō said. "Unless . . ."

Ishii looked hopeful.

"I have purchased books from your guild master, Sora-*san*, for many years," the magistrate continued. "I know him for an honorable man, and do not believe he would pledge his life on behalf of a man he does not trust. Therefore, if he agrees to act as guarantor, I will release Ishii-*san* into his custody until the trial resumes."

Ishii looked over his shoulder. "Kintaro—go find Sora-*san*."

The words had barely left his lips when the child took off running.

A surprisingly short time later, Kintaro returned in the company of a slender, middle-aged man in a striped kimono. The guild master stood almost as tall as Father Mateo, and moved with a natural grace that suggested confidence.

Kintaro returned to Hiro's side like a bird returning to its nest, but Sora continued forward to the edge of the shirazu where Ishii still knelt.

"Good morning, Sora-*san*," the magistrate said. "Did the child explain the reason for my summons?"

Sora bowed. "With apologies for my ignorance, he mentioned only that it was an urgent matter."

The magistrate explained the situation. "However, this is a proposal, not a mandate. If you have the least concern about this man"— Magistrate Hōjō gestured to Ishii—"then I expect you to refuse, and we will lock him up until the trial."

"I regret this inconvenience, Sora-*sama*," Ishii said, "but I give my word, I will not betray your trust."

Sora gazed thoughtfully at the kneeling man.

For several seconds, no one spoke.

At last, Sora addressed the magistrate. "I consent to serve as Ishii's guarantor. I give my oath: he will not flee before the end of the investigation."

Hiro noted the unusual choice of words.

"The law requires that you acknowledge the penalty you will bear if the accused does not appear before me when I reconvene his trial," Magistrate Hōjō said.

Sora bowed his head. "I understand that if Ishii-*san* does not appear, I must suffer the penalty in his stead."

"Then I remand Ishii-*san* to your custody until his trial resumes in one week's time. Remember: he remains accused of a crime for which the penalty is death. Watch him closely. Do not allow him to wander

freely. He must sleep in your home, and you must know his where-
abouts at every hour of the day and night."

"It will be done as you command," Sora confirmed.

The magistrate considered Father Mateo. "I have heard it said that
Kirishitans do not lie. Is this the truth?"

If you don't know, how can you trust his answer? Hiro mused.

"It is the truth," Father Mateo said, "by God's commandment."

"Good," the magistrate replied, "because if you cannot determine
the victim's identity, or how he died, I expect you to tell me so, and to
say it plainly. Like your god, I insist upon the truth."

"I understand," the Jesuit said, "and I will do so."

"All of you are dismissed, for one week's time." Magistrate Hōjō
raised his hand. "Remove this man, and bring the next case forward."

Sora and Father Mateo helped Ishii to his feet as another dōshin
led a worried-looking prisoner toward the sand.

As the group left the shirazu, Daisuke caught Hiro's eye. "Matsui-
san, may I have a word in private?"

Father Mateo raised his eyebrows in a silent question as the commander of the fire brigade turned on his heel and walked away.

"I guarantee I won't be long," Hiro said in Portuguese, and started
off after Daisuke.

As he followed the other shinobi to an empty place at the far end
of the yard, Hiro wondered what Daisuke considered safe enough to
say in public but too confidential for the priest to hear.

CHAPTER 13

When they reached the distant corner of the yard, Daisuke gave Hiro an expectant look.

Hiro did not respond.

After several awkward seconds, Daisuke demanded, "Don't you intend to ask what I want to tell you?"

"It stands to reason that you will tell me, whether or not I ask."

Anger briefly darkened Daisuke's eyes, like a cloud passing over the sun. "If anyone asks what we talked about, you tell them that I wanted you to swear an oath that your foreign master will comply with the laws of Edo."

"Is that the best cover story you can manage?" Hiro sighed. "Fine. I agree to say you requested such an oath—but I will not say I made one."

Daisuke scowled. "I should have known. You were always non-compliant. Even as a child."

Hiro watched the larger man impassively. In his experience, few things irritated bullies more than failing to elicit a response.

"There are things you need to know before you start your investigation. Most importantly: the body in the fire was one of us."

"I expected that, or something similar," Hiro said. "How did you know?"

"The smith may not have recognized the marks on the swords, but I did—and I think you would as well. They were forged in Iga."

"Do you know who they belonged to?" Hiro asked.

"In Edo, he was known as Yasuari."

Hiro gave no indication that he recognized the name. "Did you know him?"

"Only that he served the daimyō." Daisuke glanced toward the magistrate's dais. "Obviously, I could not mention it, because the commander of the fire brigade would have no cause to know."

"Too dangerous to mention, but safe enough to discuss in an open yard?"

"Would you have agreed to meet me alone, in a private location?" Daisuke did not wait for an answer. "I needed you to know at once, so you could ensure your foreign master keeps his mouth shut while he's looking for the truth."

"Do you know who murdered Yasuari?" Hiro asked.

"Given our talk last night, I know who I suspect." Daisuke looked across the yard, to where Hiyoshi was removing the last of the rope from around Ishii's wrists.

The bookbinder rubbed his hands together. Sora said something to Kintaro, though the intervening distance made his words impossible to hear.

"Ishii?" Hiro found that difficult to believe. "I know the corpse was in his shop, but . . ."

"Don't tell me you believe his claims of innocence?" Daisuke made a disparaging noise. "He said precisely what a guilty man would say."

"And if he's not the killer?" Hiro asked.

"Then you and the priest had better find out who is, and be sure to tell me what you learn before you tell the magistrate. If Oda's spies are responsible, I want to be the one who makes them pay for what they did to Yasuari."

"Have you found any other evidence that you have not revealed?" Hiro asked.

"Just this." Daisuke slipped his hand into his obi and withdrew it, clutched into a fist.

He opened his fingers to reveal a small, dark object the size of a chestnut. "I found it early this morning, in the ruins of the fire."

It looked like a rabbit, carved from rust-streaked stone.

"Is that a hare?" Hiro asked.

"It's how I knew for certain that the corpse was Yasuari. This *netsuke* belonged to his father. Yasuari carried it with him everywhere."

"You are certain that it's his, and not just similar?" Hiro asked.

Daisuke closed his hand around the little hare. "There's no mistake." He returned the object to his obi quickly, and switched to far more formal Japanese. "I sincerely appreciate your kind understanding of this most delicate situation, Matsui-*san*."

Footsteps thumped the earth behind Hiro as Hiyoshi joined them.

"Is this ronin causing trouble?" Hiyoshi asked.

"Not at all," Daisuke said. "I merely wanted to ensure his master understands the law. As I mentioned, Matsui-*san,* my men and I are at your disposal. I will take no more of your valuable time for now."

Hiyoshi looked disappointed. "Well, then. I will go and report to Yoriki Sato. He will want to know about the hearing."

"Watch out for him," Daisuke warned Hiro softly as the dōshin walked away. "He likes to interfere—almost as much as he likes the sound of his own voice."

Hiro returned to Father Mateo, who stood waiting with Sora and Ishii.

Daisuke continued past them with a nod. As the large man reached the gate to the magistrate's yard, Ryun and the other firefighter fell in step behind him like a pair of hunting dogs on their master's heels, and the three of them disappeared into the street.

Sora bowed to Hiro and the priest. "Thank you for agreeing to conduct the investigation, even though our problems are not your concern. With apologies for my rudeness, I do need to return to my shop."

"Yes, thank you for your kind assistance," Ishii said. "I am truly grateful."

"Could I talk with you on the way?" the Jesuit suggested. "I have some questions I would like to ask."

"I am happy to oblige," Sora replied, "although . . . I doubt I have any useful information."

The tall man's pause made Hiro doubt his words.

Sora started toward the gate with Father Mateo at his side. Hiro followed with Ishii, a step behind.

"I wish to show proper respect for your position as the head of the booksellers' guild," Father Mateo said. "Should I refer to you as 'Master Sora'?"

The tall man cast a worried glance at the samurai on guard beside the gates. "With respect, we have not obtained the required permission from the daimyō, and are not yet officially a guild. At this time, we merely constitute a voluntary association—the first step toward formal recognition." He lowered his voice. "I am allowed to use the title 'master' in some contexts, but I do not wish to seem as if I claim a right beyond my station. 'Sora-*san*' is more than adequate."

"Of course." Father Mateo glanced over his shoulder. "Ishii-*san*, did you suspect the recent fires might be connected at any time before your shop caught fire?"

"Not for a moment," the bookbinder replied. "Everyone agreed the fires were accidents. Although, until two months ago, it had been over a year since a book-related shop caught fire. The rules are working, Sora-*san*."

"To my great relief," Sora said.

"What rules?" Father Mateo asked.

"When I became the leader of our fledgling guild—" Sora dipped his head in embarrassment. "I admit, we use the term among ourselves, if not in public. At that time, I instituted several rules designed to prevent the start and spread of fires. Despite the initial arguments it caused, we have—or had, until recently—the best safety record in all of Edo."

"And yet, the recent fires did not make you suspicious?" Hiro asked.

"If you had known the men involved . . ." Sora shook his head. "My primary concern was poor Kintaro."

Hiro looked around. "Speaking of the boy . . . where has he gone?"

CHAPTER 14

"I sent him back to my shop, to warn my wife about what happened." Sora shook his head. "The boy has suffered more than anyone from the recent fires. The calligrapher killed in the first fire was his father, and Kintaro also was Goro-*san*'s apprentice. I apologize— Goro-*san* was the carver whose shop burned down last week."

"I thought the boy was Ishii-*san*'s apprentice," Father Mateo said.

"He became my apprentice just last week," Ishii replied, "on the day of Goro's execution."

"Are the fire brigade and the magistrate aware of this information?" Hiro asked.

Sora rounded a busy corner, stepped to the side of the road and stopped, as if the response required his full attention. "You suspect Kintaro caused the fires."

Hiro raised his eyebrows but said nothing.

Sora continued firmly, "The boy is a victim, not the cause. He was not present when the fire destroyed his father's home. As for the second fire . . . Goro-*san* was a talented artisan, but I have never known a more slovenly man. I thought an apprentice would help him keep his workshop clean, but he used the boy as an excuse to make a larger mess than he did before."

"Had I suspected the boy at all, I never would have agreed to take him in," Ishii declared.

"Even so," Hiro said, "you must admit it looks suspicious."

"A child?" Father Mateo's tone and expression made it clear the priest did not agree.

"I would be glad to discuss this with you further," Sora said, "but my shop is just ahead, and I would prefer to speak where Kintaro has no chance to overhear."

"Forgive my presumption, Sora-*san*," Ishii put in, "but if you wish, you could continue your conversation here. I can go ahead to the shop and assist any customers on your behalf, and keep an eye on Kintaro also. As you can see the shop from here, I do not think the magistrate would mind."

"Thank you, Ishii," Sora said.

"Of course." The bookbinder bowed to Father Mateo and then to Hiro. "Please excuse me. Thank you again for coming to my aid."

He rejoined the flow of pedestrian traffic and continued down the street until he reached a large shop at the center of the block. The tall wooden shutters across the front of the store were folded open, giving passersby an unobstructed view of the interior. The floor of the shop itself stood slightly less than knee-high off the ground, and a low wooden step ran all the way across the front. Two pairs of well-worn sandals, one of them in a child's size, sat at the near end of the wooden step. Just inside the shop itself, low wooden tables held an alluring array of books and ledgers.

Hiro watched as Ishii left his sandals on the step and entered the store.

"You left the shop open?" Father Mateo asked.

"Eiko-*san* can manage for a short time in my absence," Sora said, "although we have an infant son, so I do not like to burden her."

"We will not delay you long," Father Mateo said.

"Have you considered the possibility that Kintaro might have started the fires?" Hiro's question drew a look of disapproval from the priest.

"Of course, I noted the boy's connection to the fires when they occurred." Sora remained polite, but firm. "However, I assure you it is purely coincidental."

"Did you inform the fire brigade, or the magistrate?" Hiro asked.

"As it happens, I chose to withhold that information. I feared they would draw the same mistaken conclusion you have drawn, and the boy has suffered enough. With respect, I know the child, and you do not. He did not start these fires."

"Of course not," Father Mateo said. "Hiro and I would never blame a child. And I apologize for my scribe's suspicious nature."

"Please understand," Sora said, "I have known Kintaro almost all his life. I find it impossible to believe that he would start even a single fire, to say nothing of three.

"Kintaro's mother died two years ago, and after that his father— Kenji—tried to raise the boy alone. Unfortunately, her death affected Kenji-*san* too greatly, and his grief did not abate. Eventually, he sought solace in poppy tears. His calligraphy suffered. Kintaro suffered too.

"I spoke with the apothecaries' guild, as well as Kenji, and he promised to stop smoking poppy tears. The apothecaries refused to sell them to him anymore and, for a while, I thought he was improving.

"Then, about four months ago, I passed Kintaro sitting in the street, in tears. At first, he refused to tell me what was wrong, but eventually he admitted that he had not eaten in three days. His father had returned to the poppy tears."

"Where did he get them?" Father Mateo asked.

"I do not know. I suspect the woman, but no one seems to know who she was, either."

"The one who perished with him, in the fire?" Father Mateo asked.

Sora nodded. "We tried to discover her identity, but failed. We do not think she lived in Edo. Both Kintaro and the neighbors said she only visited Kenji-*san* at night, so the fire brigade concluded that she must have been a prostitute.

"The day I found Kintaro in the street, I made Kenji consent to the boy becoming an apprentice. Ordinarily, I would have waited for another year or two, but given the circumstances . . . fortunately, Goro-*san* agreed to take the boy at once."

"Did Kintaro object to leaving his father's home?" Father Mateo asked.

"Not to me," Sora said, "although I suspect the truth is far more complicated than a simple 'yes' or 'no.' Kintaro loved his father deeply, and, despite his failings, Kenji loved Kintaro in return.

"I do not know how the fires began, but I know Kintaro did

not start them." Sora gestured to his shop. "I would never allow him underneath my roof, with my wife and infant son, if I thought that he presented any danger."

"Even so," Hiro said, "we will need to speak with the boy alone."

"I understand. But, when you do, I hope you will remember that he is a child, and one who has suffered deeply painful losses."

"I assure you, no one will mistreat him," Father Mateo said.

Hiro changed the subject. "Do you know of anyone who held a grudge against your association, or the members of it?"

Sora considered the question before he spoke. "No. We make and sell books. We cause no harm."

"And the dead man in the fire?" Hiro asked. "What do you know of him?"

"Nothing more than what the magistrate said this morning." Sora paused. "For what it's worth, I do not think Ishii-*san* killed him. If you wish, I can provide you with a list of the artisans in my association. Perhaps one of them knows something useful."

"One of whom?" Hiyoshi appeared at Hiro's side. He squinted at each of them in turn. "Where is Ishii? You gave your word he would not escape, but he has disappeared already!"

"With respect, he has not disappeared," Sora replied. "I sent him ahead, to my shop, so I could speak with the investigators privately."

Hiro noted the slight emphasis on the final word.

"You had better tell them everything you know about these fires," Hiyoshi threatened. "If another shop burns down and sets the neighboring homes ablaze, or if people die, the daimyō will never recognize your guild. In fact, he will expel the lot of you from Edo."

"Surely the daimyō would not blame an entire guild for events they could not control," Father Mateo said.

"You speak like a man who does not understand the threat of fire, or the importance of this investigation." Hiyoshi puffed out his chest. "If Magistrate Hōjō had put me in charge, I would not be standing around like a noodle vendor, wasting time. I would be searching for important evidence."

"As it happens," the Jesuit began, "we were trying—"

Hiyoshi spoke over him. "You do not know what to do, because you don't know Edo or its merchants. Fortunately, I have come to help you."

"How very thoughtful," the priest said drily.

Hiyoshi did not seem to hear him. "I will show you where to go and who to talk to. I will even help you ask the questions."

"Please excuse me." Sora bowed. "I must return to my shop . . . and watch Ishii."

Hiyoshi gave a dismissive nod. As Sora departed, the dōshin fixed his gaze on Father Mateo. "Now, as I have graciously agreed to help, I believe you owe me something in return."

"Have you something specific in mind?" Hiro asked, on the priest's behalf.

"When we learn the truth about the fire, and catch the samurai's killer, you will tell Daisuke-*san* that I solved the case."

"Daisuke—not the magistrate?" Hiro found that interesting.

"I do not care who gets the credit with the magistrate," Hiyoshi said. "Daisuke-*san* is the one with the power to let me join the fire brigade."

CHAPTER 15

"You have wanted to join the fire brigade for quite some time," the Jesuit observed.

"Daisuke-*san* does not appreciate my worth. I am a skilled investigator, and I understand the causes of fires. I have been studying." Hiyoshi leaned forward and lowered his voice. "They speak, you know. The fires. When they burn. If you know how to listen, they will tell you many things."

"You can hear the fires speaking?" Hiro asked.

"Sometimes. Not well, yet. But I am learning. Unfortunately, I cannot help with investigations now unless Daisuke-*san* asks for my assistance. Which he does not do." Hiyoshi frowned. "My current work is boring. No one likes the police. But everyone likes the fire brigade."

"The men on the fire brigade are commoners." Hiro feigned a sneer on the final word. "Even their commander, although samurai by birth, has lower status than a real warrior."

Or even a dōshin, Hiro thought, but did not say.

"People respect the fire brigade." Hiyoshi squinted at Hiro and added, "No one respects a ronin."

"I respect all men," Father Mateo said. "And I agree to your condition. When we find the killer, Hiro and I will tell Daisuke that you solved the case."

"You will?" Hiyoshi gave the priest a startled look. "Well then. I will teach you how to understand a fire, and how we investigate them here in Edo. First, we will speak with the other men in Sora's guild." He lowered his voice again. "As you know, they are not truly a guild, but they will cooperate more fully if we humor them in this regard."

"You think we should start with the other artisans?" Hiro asked. "Not with Ishii?"

"The bookbinder?" Hiyoshi shook his head. "A novice error. The men and women whose shops catch fire are never helpful. They always lie, in a futile attempt to save themselves from punishment. It never works, but they always try."

"If the law was just, they would not need to lie," Father Mateo said.

"Do not blame the law," Hiyoshi replied. "People lie because it is their nature. That's enough talking. Follow me."

He started down the street away from Sora's shop. Father Mateo glanced at Hiro, shrugged, and followed.

Hiro would have preferred to start with Ishii and Kintaro, but as he had no desire to include Hiyoshi in those conversations, he fell in step behind the dōshin and the priest.

"Hiyoshi-*san*," Father Mateo asked, "have you any ideas about the identity of the samurai who perished in the fire?"

"I do not believe he died in the fire," the dōshin said. "I think that he was dead before it started."

Father Mateo began to speak, but Hiyoshi continued, "When a fire breaks out in an artisan's shop, it is important to speak with the other members of the guild. Often, they can offer helpful information. As I mentioned, the bookmakers and booksellers are not yet an official guild, but many people believe they will receive recognition soon.

"The demand for books is growing fast. I do not read, myself, but most of the samurai I know have started collecting books. Many artisans buy them too. Last week, I even saw a *farmer* buy a book." He raised his hands. "Can you believe it? Farmers, reading books!"

"It sounds like a fine idea to me," Father Mateo said.

Hiyoshi continued as if the Jesuit had not spoken. "I saw him carrying it down the street, and thought he stole it. I stopped him and said 'What are you doing? Why did you steal that book?' He said he bought it, but I am not that easy to fool. I made him return it to the shop. That's when the shopkeeper explained the farmer had paid for it. A farmer with a book! Have you ever heard of such a thing?"

He squinted at Father Mateo expectantly.

The Jesuit seemed about to answer but, instead, asked, "How long have you wanted to join the fire brigade?"

"I wanted to apply for Daisuke-*sama*'s position when the daimyō created it, ten years ago." Hiyoshi frowned. "My father insisted I join him in the police instead."

"What made your father change his mind?" the Jesuit asked.

"He did not change his mind," Hiyoshi said. "He died. I applied to join the fire brigade the very day my year of mourning ended, and twice more since. I do not understand why Daisuke-*sama* keeps refusing my petitions. In one breath, he claims Ryuu-*san* is the only assistant he requires, but with the next, he tells the magistrate he has no time. No matter. I will prove my worth in this investigation. Then Daisuke-*sama* will change his mind."

Hiro put no faith in either of those assumptions.

"After my father died," Hiyoshi continued, "I rented a room in a row house near the fire watch tower. That way, I can hear the alarms even at night. I follow the fire brigade to every fire, day and night. Except for the ones that happen when I do my work for the police, of course. In this way, I have proven my loyalty and fortitude. Now, I will prove I can do the work as well."

He gave Father Mateo a suspicious look. "How long do you intend to stay in Edo?"

"Only long enough to complete the investigation. Matsui-*san* and I have business waiting in the south."

Hiro wondered whether Father Mateo actually intended to comply with Hanzō's original instructions and go to the Portuguese colony at Yokoseura when their mission was complete. Given the Jesuit's artful phrasing, and their previous discussions on the topic, Hiro doubted it—but admired the priest's ability to obfuscate while speaking only truth.

"Then you don't plan to stay and steal my place on the fire brigade," Hiyoshi said.

"Have no fear," the priest replied, "I have no desire to join the Edo fire brigade. Or any other, for that matter."

Hiyoshi stopped in front of a one-story building with a sloping tiled roof. A dusty noren hung across the door. "The calligrapher who owns this shop writes Buddhist sutras. He's a priest himself, so people trust him and tell him things. Listen carefully while I ask him questions. You will learn how a skilled investigator gathers evidence about a crime."

Three hours and numerous conversations later, Hiyoshi, Hiro, and Father Mateo had spoken with every member of Sora's guild. At every shop, Hiyoshi had explained about the fire, and how he intended to solve the crime and earn a place on the fire brigade, in great detail. He insisted on conducting all the interviews himself, talked far too much, and asked only simple, straightforward questions. The artisans treated him with polite but tired respect, making Hiro suspect they knew Hiyoshi well. They answered his questions openly, but had no useful information, either about the fire in Ishii's shop or the two that occurred before.

The final interview involved an elderly maker of woodblock prints, whose shop was next to the empty lot where Goro's shop once stood. The old man clearly wanted to assist them, but had nothing new to tell.

When the interview concluded, Hiro and Father Mateo followed Hiyoshi back into the street.

"I don't understand." The dōshin glared at the empty, burned out lot. "We talked with everyone, but no one knows what happened."

"It's more common than you might believe," Father Mateo said.

"I do not believe it," Hiyoshi declared. "Someone in Edo knows what happened in Ishii-*san*'s shop, and how the fire began. Commoners are liars. They don't understand the danger. Sooner or later, a fire will destroy this entire city. They'll be sorry then!"

Behind them, the noren in the entrance to the printmaker's shop fluttered open and the elderly artisan emerged. He looked around until he located Hiro and the others. He started toward them, wiping his hands on his faded, dusty apron.

As the noren closed behind him, a hand pulled it aside, revealing the old man's wife—a gray-haired woman who wore a faded kimono and a determined frown. She stood in the doorway and crossed her arms, staring after her husband like a mother supervising an errant child.

When the elderly artisan reached Hiyoshi, he bent in a deep, respectful bow. "Pardon me, Honorable Dōshin." He straightened and waited for permission to continue.

"What do you want?" Hiyoshi asked.

"I apologize for interrupting you, but my wife"—he gestured to the woman watching them from the doorway—"wants me to share some additional information about the fire."

CHAPTER 16

"You have more information about the fire?" Hiyoshi asked. "Why didn't you mention this before?"

"With apologies," the old man said, "this information relates to the fire at Goro-*san's* establishment, two weeks ago . . . and we did mention it to the fire brigade, during their investigation of that fire."

"I distinctly asked if you knew of anything that might assist my investigation." Hiyoshi's voice grew louder as he spoke. "You said that you did not. You lied!"

"With respect," the elderly printmaker said, "you asked about new information, and this information is not new. However, my wife agrees that—"

"Your wife is a commoner!" Hiyoshi declared. "Commoners have no right to agree or disagree. They merely obey the commands of samurai."

"Forgive me," Father Mateo said. "What is your honorable name?"

"I am called Susumu," the printmaker said.

"We appreciate your diligence, Susumu-*san*," the priest replied, "and your wife's as well. We will gladly return and speak with her."

"No need for that," Susumu said. "She sent me out to speak on her behalf. She thinks you need to know that we smelled camphor on the night the fire broke out in Goro's shop."

"You smelled camphor?" Hiyoshi looked confused.

"*She* smelled it." Susumu tilted his head in his wife's direction. "At my age, I can't smell anything anymore. But I've been married for more years than I can count, and if my wife says 'we' smelled camphor, I know better than to argue."

Hiro stifled a smile.

"Why should we care if your wife smelled camphor?" Hiyoshi asked.

"Camphor wood is flammable," Father Mateo said.

The dōshin made a dismissive sound. "All wood is flammable."

"True," Hiro said, "but camphor oil, and camphor paste, can explode when exposed to heat or flame. Did Goro's shop explode?"

He resisted the urge to add *also*.

"No. In fact, the fire started quietly." Susumu gestured toward the place where his wife stood watching from the entrance to his shop. "Goro-*san* walked over to visit me that evening, as he often did after he closed his shop. It was snowing that night, so we stood inside my shop and talked. A few minutes later, we saw the flames, and realized his shop had caught on fire."

"Was your wife there when this happened?" Father Mateo asked.

Susumu shook his head. "She left for a walk as soon as Goro-*san* arrived."

"When and where does she think she smelled the camphor?" Hiro asked.

"She said she smelled it when Goro-*san* arrived, and in the air when she left for her walk. To be clear, I have no doubt she smelled it. Goro-*san* suffered from pain in his hands and fingers, especially in winter." Susumu rubbed his own bony hands together. "The apothecary gave him camphor paste to help the pain. He said it helped so much. I wanted some myself, but my wife says the odor clung to Goro-*san* like a baby monkey on its mother's back, she said—"

Hiyoshi waved a dismissive hand. "We understand. She hated camphor. No one cares. Do you have any *useful* information we should know?"

"Only that my wife thinks Goro-*san* left camphor paste too close to an open flame, and that's how the fire began. If I recall, the magistrate agreed. But . . ."

"Do you disagree with that assessment?" Hiro asked.

"I knew Goro-*san* for many years," Susumu said. "We trained together, set our shops up side by side. He produced some of the highest quality blocks and prints in Edo. But even though I admired his work, and also considered him a friend, I can admit . . . his shop was dangerous."

"Dangerous?" the Jesuit repeated.

"Unclean does not begin to describe it properly," Susumu said. "He refused to clean, or even clear away the shavings, until they piled up so high he could not work. When Sora-*san* required him take an apprentice, Goro made the poor boy do all the cleaning work on his behalf."

"You mean Kintaro," Father Mateo said.

The old man nodded. "To his credit, the boy worked hard and tried to keep the shop in a better state. There was simply nothing he could do—"

"Enough!" Hiyoshi interrupted. "I am an important man. Do you think I have nothing better to do than stand here listening to you all day? No one reported the scent of camphor in the air around Ishii-*san*'s shop."

"I don't know anything about that fire," Susumu said. "I just—"

"This will not help me gain a place on the fire brigade." Hiyoshi waved a hand. "Go away, old man. You waste my time."

Susumu bowed. "I apologize."

"Please thank your wife for her diligence and concern," Father Mateo said.

Susumu gave the priest a grateful smile as he started back toward his shop.

"You should not have thanked him," Hiyoshi grumbled. "My favorite restaurant had a sign beside the door—they had fresh eels today, and now I'm going to miss them, all because of an old man's rambling."

Hiro noted the position of the sun, high overhead. "You might still get some, if you leave right now."

"You cannot solve this crime without me," Hiyoshi said. "You need my help."

"Even so," Hiro said, "I see no harm in taking a break to eat."

"I agree," Father Mateo added. "In fact, we might as well take the rest of the afternoon off, and start again tomorrow morning."

"We have not spoken with the boy," Hiyoshi said, "or with Ishii, although, as I explained to you before, he will only lie. Now that you mention it, I have worked hard this morning. I deserve a rest and a filling meal. If I hurry . . ." He squinted at the Jesuit. "Can foreigners eat eels?"

"I can . . ." Father Mateo glanced at Hiro. "But the restaurant might not have three servings left. I am sure fresh eels are very popular."

"Especially in winter," Hiyoshi said.

"You have helped us greatly. You deserve a special treat." Father Mateo bowed. "Please go and enjoy your eels. I need to say my midday prayers anyway."

"Very well, but come and find me when you're ready to resume the investigation," Hiyoshi said. "I am available to help you any time of the day or night."

He did not wait for an answer, or even bow, before he hurried off.

"Thank you for that," Hiro said as soon as Hiyoshi was out of earshot.

Father Mateo smiled. "I know how you feel about eels."

"It's not only the eels." Hiro started off in the direction of Sora's shop, which fortunately stood in a different direction from the one Hiyoshi chose. "I don't want him around when we talk with Kintaro."

"Kintaro—not Ishii?"

"I don't believe we can learn anything more from Ishii at this point, but the boy is another matter."

"Do you think Kintaro set the fires?" Father Mateo asked abruptly.

"At the moment, I consider it merely a strange coincidence that requires investigation."

"I will not send a child to his death," the priest declared.

"No one has proposed that," Hiro said. "However, if—"

"Do not even say it," Father Mateo ordered. "A child of ten could not kill a shinobi. For that reason, if no other, it is clear the boy was not involved."

Unless the boy is also shinobi, Hiro thought, but since Kintaro showed no signs of special training—and would have been retrieved by another member of his clan after his father's death, had he belonged to a shinobi ryu—he chose to change the subject. "Daisuke confirmed the dead man was a member of the Iga ryu."

"Is that what he told you in the magistrate's yard?" Father Mateo asked.

Hiro recounted the details of his conversation with Daisuke. When he finished, Father Mateo said, "Does he have any evidence suggesting that Ishii is a spy?"

"Not that he mentioned," Hiro said. "And if he did, I believe—"

"—he would have killed the bookbinder himself," Father Mateo finished.

"More likely than not," Hiro confirmed. "But even the best of spies cannot always conceal his nature from the people he lives with."

"Then I suppose we should speak with Kintaro, after all."

CHAPTER 17

Sora sat near the entrance to his shop, reading a book. When he heard Hiro and Father Mateo's footsteps he looked up, jumped to his feet, and bowed.

"Good afternoon gentlemen. How may I assist you?"

"We wish to speak with Kintaro," Hiro said.

"He . . ." Sora glanced toward the empty back of the shop. His voice dropped to a whisper as a flush spread up his cheeks. "He is not here. Eiko—my wife—refused to let him stay. I tried to persuade her that the fires were mere coincidences, but she would not listen."

"She believes Kintaro was involved?" Father Mateo asked.

"Not precisely," Sora said. "She thinks the kami bear a grudge against the boy, and that misfortune shadows his every step. She fears his presence in our home will bring the wrath of the kami down upon us."

"Where is he now?" The Jesuit's tone conveyed his disapproval.

Sora set his book on a nearby table. "My sister, Yuki, lives in a row house near the Great River, several blocks from here. Unlike my wife, she does not suffer from an excess of superstition. She agreed to let Kintaro stay with her."

"Will you take us there?" Father Mateo asked.

Sora's flush grew deeper. "Eiko made me promise . . . you must understand, she truly believes that any contact with the boy is dangerous. I don't believe such things myself, of course, but . . ."

"Perhaps you can give us directions to your sister's home, instead?" Hiro suggested.

Relief washed over the guild master's face as he told them where to go. "You will have no trouble finding Yuki's home," he finished. "If you get lost, ask anyone in the area. Not many women live alone in Edo, and my sister is unusually independent. Trust me. Everyone in that neighborhood knows Yuki-*san*."

Hiro and Father Mateo followed Sora's directions to the proper neighborhood and street. Long row houses, one story high and oriented on a north-south axis, filled the blocks between the booksellers' district and the river. Each wooden building was composed of eight or ten individual, but connected, one-room dwellings that shared a common roof and at least two interior walls. Half of the units opened off the east side of the building, while the other half faced west. Alleys in between the houses offered enough space for several people to walk abreast, but not quite enough room for a cart to pass with ease.

Father Mateo shook his head as he and Hiro started up the passage beside the house where Sora's sister lived.

"Is something wrong?" Hiro looked at the narrow alley, trying to determine what had caused the Jesuit's reaction.

Most of the wooden doors stood open to let in light and air. Thin streams of smoke rose from the chimney openings in the roof, perfuming the air with the musk of many fires. Men and women sat on wooden stools outside the open doors, enjoying the winter sun or keeping an eye on the half-dozen toddlers waddling in the narrow space.

Father Mateo raised his scarred left hand in a gesture that encompassed the whole scene. "In Portugal, in a place like this, the filth would fill the streets. The residents would live in misery. They would die young, of starvation or disease. Here, even the alleyways are clean. The children and the elderly look fed. It is . . . a different world." He stepped around a little child who gaped at him in fascination.

"With apologies," Hiro said, "your former home does not sound pleasant."

Father Mateo shrugged and did not respond.

A tall, thin woman emerged from the final doorway at the far end of the row house on the right. She wore a gold kimono and an obi in a muted shade of violet. Although not beautiful, her face fell into patient, pleasant lines. She reached for a broom that stood beside the door and swept the alley near her home.

Hiro gestured in her direction. "That will be Yuki."

"How do you know?" Father Mateo asked.

"Sora said 'the last room on the right,' but even without that, she is the only woman here of Sora's height."

She looked up as they approached.

"Good morning," Father Mateo said. "Are you Yuki-*san*?"

"I am." A guarded expression fell across her face as she executed a graceful bow. "May I help you with something?"

The Jesuit introduced himself and Hiro. "Magistrate Hōjō asked us to investigate the fire that took place last night. We have come to speak with young Kintaro."

Yuki rested her broom against the wall beside the door and brushed her hands together to remove any lingering dust. "While I respect your request, Kintaro-*kun* is but a child, and was apprenticed to Ishii-*san* just a week ago. I fail to see how he could have any useful information."

"In that case, the conversation will be short," Hiro replied.

"We merely wish to confirm what the boy may know," Father Mateo said.

"If Kintaro talks about the recent events, he will re-live them." Yuki fixed her gaze on the Jesuit. "Children experience trauma differently than adults do. You ask for a conversation. But for him, it will be terrifying."

"You seem to know a great deal about children. Have you many of your own?" Hiro looked past her, through the open doorway of her one-room home.

The modest dwelling had a narrow earthen entry with a small clay stove that squatted next to an empty sandal rack. Beyond the *genkan*, a knee-high platform eight tatami mats in size made up the rest of the woman's home. It had no windows, and no furniture except for a small, low table and a set of storage chests against the wall directly opposite the door.

Yuki followed Hiro's gaze. "Although my home may seem small to a samurai, I assure you, it is more than adequate for my needs, and for Kintaro's also. To answer your question, no. I have no husband and no children."

Her tone requested no sympathy and suggested no remorse.

"Where is the boy?" Hiro asked.

"He went to the well for water." Yuki gestured toward the open yard at the center of the block.

"May we wait for him to return?" Father Mateo asked.

"I have no authority over samurai," Yuki replied, her pleasant tone defusing any insult her words might have carried.

Hiro resisted the urge to raise an eyebrow at the woman, who walked the line between insolence and courtesy with a flair most people—let alone female commoners—would not dare.

"Do you know anything about the fire?" Hiro asked.

"With respect, would it matter if I did? The law is clear."

"Do I sense disapproval in your tone?" Hiro found this woman increasingly intriguing.

In an instant, Yuki's expression changed from irritation to amusement. "I am a woman without a husband. My opinions are entirely irrelevant."

"Not to us," Father Mateo said.

"Then you, also, are unique." She regarded him thoughtfully. "As it happens, I do not agree with executing men for negligence, and the law seems especially cruel in Ishii-san's case. I understand that, in the year since he moved to Edo, he has never once allowed an open flame inside his home or shop, except for a small fire in the stove on the earthen floor—and he stays in the room the entire time it burns. I know no person who goes to greater lengths when it comes to fire, although I suspect that safety was not his only motive. He often complained to Sora-san about the costs of fuel and candles."

"Did Ishii-*san* have financial troubles?" Father Mateo asked.

"Any answer I could give would be entirely conjecture. Aside from my brother, no man would discuss such things with me."

"But Ishii did speak to you about the price of fuel," Hiro said.

"Not to me," Yuki corrected. "However, he discusses the topic frequently with Sora-*san*, and as I often help my brother's wife cook meals, and serve them, when Sora-*san* has company, I have ample opportunity to hear their conversations."

"Do you help because she's busy with the baby?" Father Mateo asked.

"If you asked, she would likely tell you it is I who requires help." Yuki's gaze shifted up the alley. "It appears Kintaro has returned."

CHAPTER 18

Kintaro carried a wooden bucket filled to the brim with water. He wove through the other children in the alley with a practiced gait and did not spill a drop.

Yuki lowered her voice to a whisper. "When you speak with him, please, be kind."

Father Mateo dipped his head. "I give you my word, we will."

When the boy arrived, Yuki relieved him of the bucket. "Thank you for your help, Kintaro-*san*."

He looked up as if to respond, but froze at the sight of Hiro and the priest.

"Good afternoon, Kintaro," Father Mateo said. "We would like to talk with you about last night."

Kintaro bent in a deep, respectful bow. When he straightened, he kept his gaze fixed firmly on the ground.

"Please excuse me." Yuki bowed politely, gave Father Mateo a warning look, and carried the bucket of water into her home.

Kintaro clasped his hands and waited, staring at the ground.

Father Mateo looked at Hiro, who did not miss the silent plea for help in the Jesuit's eyes.

"Before we talk about the fire," Hiro said, "I would like your help resolving a personal problem."

The boy looked up. A spark of wary curiosity lit his eyes.

"I would like a cup of tea, and perhaps a bite to eat," Hiro continued, "but do not know Edo well. Could you suggest a reliable establishment?"

Kintaro nodded. "There's a teahouse by the river. Father took me there, sometimes, before . . ."

"Show us the way," Hiro said. "I will buy you a cup of tea and a snack as well."

Kintaro led Hiro and Father Mateo through the open yard at the center of the block and down another narrow alley to a wider street beyond.

"Clearly, men of noble rank don't walk these alleys often," Father Mateo murmured in Portuguese, as they passed through a gauntlet of startled looks and nervous stares.

More likely, they have never seen a foreigner, Hiro thought.

Eventually, the curving street intersected a sunny, earthen path that paralleled the largest river Hiro had seen in Edo. It flowed so wide and deep, the water looked almost black. The banks rose high and steep on either side, a testament to the river's course and volume.

"Please be careful on this path," Kintaro said as he started south along it. "If you fall in the river, and there's not a fisherman right there to save you, you will drown."

Hiro heard the echo of a parent's earnest warning in the words.

He also noted that, as hoped, the child's fear had dissipated when the topic changed to tea.

A wooden bridge arched high above the water, leaving room for fishing skiffs to pass beneath. Beyond it, several one-story wooden buildings perched on the riverbank like turtles soaking up the winter sun. Columns of fragrant smoke rose from the vents in the buildings' roofs, filling the chilly air with the tantalizing scents of grilling fish and steaming dumplings.

Kintaro slowed his pace as they reached the first house in the row. Although old, the façade looked clean and recently repaired. A crisp, two-paneled noren hung in the entrance. Bold calligraphy flowed down the right-hand panel like a waterfall of ink.

"Can you read that?" Father Mateo nodded to the noren.

"It says 'our tea is expensive,'" Hiro answered.

"What?"

Hiro smiled. "It *says* 'Great River Teahouse,' but between the prime location and the quality of the writing on that noren . . ."

"I promise, it is not expensive." Kintaro looked worried. "But I can find another teahouse, if you wish."

"This will do nicely." Hiro gave the boy an encouraging smile. "It appears to be precisely what I wanted."

They stepped through the noren into a small genkan with a packed earth floor. The scents of tea and wood smoke filled the air, and the muted hum of peaceful conversation gave the shop a welcoming atmosphere. Several pairs of well-worn sandals sat in a row on the far side of the entry, just to the right of the sliding door that led to the shop's interior.

The door stood open, revealing part of the larger room beyond. Low wooden tables sat at intervals around the tatami-covered floor. At the center of the room, a fire burned in a sunken hearth. A decorative kettle hung above the flames, suspended by a long, thin chain that dangled from the rafters.

A shadow filled the doorway as the proprietor came to greet the new arrivals. When he noticed the foreign priest, he bowed as deeply as his ample girth allowed. "Good morning, noble gentlemen. Welcome to my humble teahouse."

As he straightened, he saw the boy. "Kintaro?"

"He recommended your establishment to us," Hiro said.

"Then I am in his debt," the proprietor answered. "Please come this way."

They followed him across the large tatami room, past several tables filled with men in merchants' robes, who faced one another across plates of sweets and pots of fragrant tea. On the far side of the teahouse, a set of painted lacquer screens created a semi-private seating area, with a peaceful view of the river through a set of floor-to-ceiling slatted windows. A lone wooden table sat at the center of the space, with rounded cushions on either side.

The teahouse owner gestured to the table. "With apologies, I have no private rooms. I hope, perhaps, this will suffice?"

"You need not even—" the priest began.

"The space is acceptable. Thank you." Hiro shot the Jesuit a warning look, moved past the proprietor, and knelt on one of the cushions that faced the river.

Father Mateo frowned, but knelt beside Hiro.

As Kintaro sat down on the far side of the table, with his back to the windows, the proprietor asked, "May I offer you tea? I have both hojicha and *sencha*."

"Which do you recommend?" Hiro asked.

"I believe, perhaps, my hojicha will not offend."

"Then we will have a pot of your finest hojicha," Hiro replied.

"Have you snacks?" Father Mateo asked. "Some sweets, perhaps?"

"Today I can offer candied persimmons, roasted chestnuts, or *harabuto mochi*."

Kintaro's eyes lit up at the mention of the treats.

"Please bring a plate of each," Father Mateo said.

The teahouse owner clasped his hands in delight. "One of each? Of course! At once!" He gave a delighted bow and hurried off.

Father Mateo switched to Portuguese. "You did not need to interrupt me."

"In fact, I did," Hiro replied in kind. "Men of samurai rank do not refuse special treatment."

"I did not wish to cause him trouble."

"You prefer to cause distress?" Hiro indicated the screens that separated them from the other patrons. "Because it would, had you insisted on sitting with merchants."

"God Himself dined with merchants and tax collectors," Father Mateo said.

"He was not samurai." Hiro crossed his arms.

Kintaro bit his lip and watched the exchange with nervous eyes. Slowly, as if hoping not to be noticed, he lowered his gaze to the tabletop. His breathing grew so shallow that his slender shoulders barely moved.

CHAPTER 19

"Kintaro-*san*, is something wrong?" Father Mateo asked in Japanese.

The child startled. "No. No, sir. It's just . . . I'm sorry. For whatever I did to anger you."

"To anger . . ." The Jesuit shook his head. "I am not angry with you. You have done nothing wrong."

Kintaro looked from the priest to Hiro, still uneasy.

"The foreigner's native tongue sometimes sounds harsh, compared with Japanese," Hiro said, "but he speaks the truth. He is not displeased—with you."

"Indeed," Father Mateo said, "and I apologize for my rudeness, in speaking a language that you do not understand."

Kintaro's jaw dropped.

Hiro saw the unspoken questions in the child's eyes.

Father Mateo apparently did too. "I understand that in Japan, young boys do not ask questions of samurai. However, strictly speaking, I am not samurai. More importantly, it is my job to answer questions."

"Even questions from me?" Kintaro tapped himself on the chest.

"If you have anything you wish to ask." Father Mateo smiled.

For once, his informality might actually work to our advantage, Hiro thought.

"Is your country very far away?" Kintaro asked. "Did you get to cross the sea in a real ship?"

"It is, and I did," Father Mateo said.

"How long did it take to get here from your land?"

"Many weeks, but we also stopped in other places on the way."

Kintaro's forehead furrowed. "Do all the people in those places speak your foreign tongue?"

"Some do," Father Mateo said, "but mostly, they speak the languages of their lands."

"How many languages are there?" Kintaro paused. "Can you speak them all?"

The Jesuit laughed. "Not even close. I don't think anyone can speak them all."

"Do they have books in your country?" Kintaro asked.

"They do. In fact, I brought some with me to Japan." A flicker of sadness passed through the Jesuit's eyes. "I had to leave most of them in Kyoto."

"I had a book once, too. My father made it for me." Kintaro scowled at the table as if struggling not to cry. "But I don't have it anymore. I never even got to finish reading it."

"I am sorry to hear that." Father Mateo's voice rang with compassion.

Kintaro took a deep breath, as if to steady himself, and continued, "It was *The Tale of Genji*. The whole book—not just a few chapters. Father copied the manuscript for a samurai, and made me a copy too, as a reward for helping him. Sometimes, I read the pages he copied back to him, aloud, to help him check them."

A clever way to teach the boy to read, Hiro thought with approval.

"May I ask what happened to your book?" Father Mateo asked.

"Father sold it." In a whisper, Kintaro added, "for poppy tears."

An awkward silence followed, after which the boy continued, in a more normal tone, "Ishii-*san* has a copy that he's binding, but he will not let me read it. He says I'm not old enough to understand *The Tale of Genji*—but he's wrong."

The teahouse owner returned, bearing a lacquered tray that held a steaming teapot, three small cups, and several plates of sweets. After setting the tray in the center of the table, he gestured to a plate that held a pyramid of bite-sized balls of mochi, grilled and covered with a thin brown glaze.

"My wife prepared these *dango* just this morning. Please accept them as a gift, in thanks for your patronage." He indicated the steaming pot. "My finest hojicha. Now, please relax and enjoy yourselves. If you require anything more, please ask."

After the proprietor left, Kintaro rose up on his knees. "May I pour you tea?"

"Yes, thank you," Father Mateo said.

Kintaro carefully set three cups in a row beside the pot. He filled the first one, set the pot on the table, and used both hands to raise and extend the cup to Father Mateo. As the priest accepted the tea, the child dipped his head politely.

The boy repeated the process with a second cup for Hiro before filling the final teacup for himself.

Hiro closed his eyes as he raised his cup to his lips and inhaled the steam. Roasting enhanced the sweetness of the tea, and the scent reminded him of autumn sun on ripening rice. He took a sip. The rich, deep flavor lingered on his tongue.

He took another sip and opened his eyes to find Kintaro watching. The boy immediately dropped his gaze to his own cup.

"This tea is delicious," Father Mateo said.

Hiro tasted it again. "I am quite pleased."

Kintaro's pale cheeks flushed pink as he sipped his tea. Although he watched the plates of sweets with eager eyes, he did not touch them.

Father Mateo gestured to the food. "Kintaro-*san*, please help yourself to anything you wish."

The boy began to reach for the plates but stopped. "You haven't eaten any yet."

The Jesuit plucked a dango from the top of the pile and popped it in his mouth. He chewed and swallowed. "I believe that solves the problem."

Kintaro's face burst into a grin as he reached for a dango of his own.

"Don't tell Ana," Father Mateo said as he selected another chewy morsel, "but these are even better than the ones she makes."

Curiosity piqued, Hiro picked up a dango. As he bit down on the bite-sized ball, the crispy outer surface yielded to the familiar, chewy texture of pounded rice. The tangy glaze filled his mouth with pleasant heat—not spicy, but delightfully complex; a perfect complement to the roasted tea.

Kintaro carefully selected a plump, golden chestnut from the bowl beside the dango. He ate it slowly, in three careful bites, with sips of tea between them.

Hiro lifted the teapot and refilled Father Mateo's cup, and then Kintaro's.

The child stared.

Hiro raised an eyebrow. "Have you never seen a samurai pour tea?"

"N-not for me." Kintaro looked at his cup as if afraid that it might bite.

"Well, now you have." Hiro set the teapot on the table. The time had come to make this conversation useful, but he needed to shift the topic gently, so as not to scare the boy. "I also read *The Tale of Genji* secretly when I was young."

"How did you know . . . are you going to tell Ishii-*san*?"

"Do you read when you should be working?" Hiro asked.

Kintaro shook his head vehemently. "Only at night, after Ishii-*san* goes to sleep."

Hiro shrugged. "Then what you read is none of my concern. Or his."

"If the book belongs to him, it would be better to obtain permission," Father Mateo said, "although I suppose it does not matter now. The book would not have survived the fire."

"But it did." Kintaro reached for another chestnut. "The book was in the storehouse, not the shop."

"Your master had a storehouse?" Hiro prompted.

Kintaro nodded as he chewed. After swallowing the chestnut, he continued, "Ishii-*san* was afraid of thieves and fire. Every night, while he cooked the meal, I had to carry all the books from the workshop to his storehouse in the next block over."

"All of them?" Hiro asked.

Kintaro bit his lip. "I was supposed to take them all. Sometimes I didn't."

CHAPTER 20

"On some nights, I hid a chapter from *The Tale of Genji*, to read when Ishii-*san* went to sleep," Kintaro confessed. "But I could only do it when the moon was close to full. On other nights, it was too dark to read."

"Is that why Ishii could not find you when the fire began last night?" Father Mateo refilled Hiro's teacup, then Kintaro's, and then his own. "Were you reading?"

"No. Last night Ishii-*san* took the books to the storehouse by himself. He made me sweep the shop instead. I was mad, but now I'm glad. *The Tale of Genji* would have been burned up."

"But you weren't sleeping when the fire began," Hiro prompted.

"I was," Kintaro said slowly, "but not where I'm supposed to sleep. Ishii-*san* snores. He's so loud, he keeps me awake. And it's hard to go to sleep so early. On some nights, it's barely even dark.

"Last night, after he went to sleep, I went into the shop. I lay down by the window. I wanted to watch the sky. Sometimes, I can see stars through the shutters. Last night, I fell asleep on the floor, waiting for the stars.

"When I woke up, there was smoke and fire. It was so hot. I couldn't breathe." Kintaro's face grew taut at the memory. "I couldn't find the door."

"Weren't you lying right beside the shutters?" Hiro asked.

"The shutters were on fire." Kintaro grew agitated. "The front of the shop, and the ceiling—everything was all on fire. I crawled to the back of the shop, but I got lost. My eyes were burning. I couldn't see anything but smoke. It hurt so much."

Tears welled up in the child's eyes. "I called for help, but no one came. So I hid in the water barrel. Well, I tried to, but I couldn't get inside."

"The water barrel?" Father Mateo asked.

"The big one, at the back of the shop. Ishii-*san* kept it there in case of fire. The fire was too big for a barrel of water to put it out, but I thought, if I hid inside—water doesn't burn, so I'd be safe. But the lid was stuck. I couldn't get it off.

"I was trying to get it open when he found me."

"Who found you?" Hiro asked, although he knew the answer.

"The commander of the fire brigade—Daisuke-*san*. He rescued me. He picked me up and ran right through the flames! So I didn't have to get in the barrel after all."

Good thing, too. Hiro decided not to mention that the boy had nearly made a deadly error. The water in the barrel would have protected him from the flames—just long enough to boil him to death.

"Have you any idea how the fire began?" Father Mateo asked. "Or where?"

Kintaro shook his head. "I was asleep."

"What about the other fires?" Hiro took unusual care to ask the question gently. "Do you remember where you were when they began?"

"Before Father died, I was living with Goro-*san*," the boy replied. "I didn't want to, but they made me. Sora-*san* and Father. Sometimes Father let me visit him, and spend the night, but not that night. He never let me stay with him when *she* came."

"She . . . you mean the woman who came to see him?" Hiro asked.

Kintaro nodded.

"Do you know who she was? Or where she lived?"

Kintaro shook his head. "Father said someday I'd get to meet her. But I never did." He gave Hiro a pleading look. "He wasn't smoking poppies any more. He stopped. He promised me. He *promised*. He was going to bring me home, and teach me to become a calligrapher, like him."

Kintaro's shoulders heaved. He closed his eyes, and tears ran down his face.

Father Mateo closed his own eyes and bowed his head in a way that made Hiro suspect the priest was praying.

After several seconds, Hiro asked, "Can you tell me anything about the night that Goro's shop caught fire?"

As he hoped, the question distracted Kintaro enough to let the boy regain control of his emotions. "I don't know how that fire started. I wasn't there. I was at Father's grave."

"All night?" Hiro asked. "Outside, in the cold?"

"I was there," Kintaro insisted. "If you don't believe me, ask my uncle. It was all his fault!"

"Of course we . . ." Father Mateo processed the child's words. "You have an uncle?"

"His name is Usaburo. He makes paper." Kintaro scowled and crossed his arms. "He hated Father, and he hates me too. But I hate him even more."

"Hate is a powerful word," the priest began.

Hiro had no time for platitudes. "Why did your uncle hate your father?"

"I don't know." Kintaro uncrossed his arms, but his anger remained. "I didn't even know I had an uncle until Father told me not to buy paper from his shop."

"How could a man you did not know cause you to spend the night at your father's grave?" Hiro asked.

The tears returned to Kintaro's eyes, and he struggled not to let them fall. "That day was the forty-ninth day after Father's death. I needed to burn incense on his grave. But Goro-*san* . . . he wouldn't give me coins to buy it." Kintaro thumped his chest with his bony fist. "They were *my* coins. I earned them. He was supposed to pay me, but he never did. Not even when I asked. So I told him he was mean and ran away. I didn't even help him close the shop."

"And you went to your uncle to ask for help," Father Mateo said.

"I thought . . ." Kintaro's scowl returned. "If I had a brother, and he died, I would *always* pay for incense for his grave. But he didn't care. He called me names. He said he hoped my Father was in hell."

Father Mateo looked appalled. "That is a terrible thing to say."

Kintaro wiped his eyes with the back of his hand. "I went to the temple and asked the Buddha to forgive my father, and forgive me too. After that, I went to Father's grave. I knelt beside it until I got too cold, and then I went inside the temple. I stayed in there, beside the Buddha, until the sun came up.

"I was afraid to go back to Goro-*san*. I thought he would beat me for the things I said. So I stayed away all night long. It was so cold, even in the temple." He looked at the Jesuit hopefully. "Do you think my suffering will help my father in the afterlife? Even though I had no incense I could burn?"

Father Mateo looked on the verge of tears, caught between his wish to comfort the grieving boy and the cardinal tenets of his faith, which offered no such comfort to nonbelievers.

Fortunately, Hiro suffered from no similar restraints. "No compassionate being—divine or otherwise—would judge your efforts and find them wanting.

"Also, the man you went to see that night is not your uncle."

"I think he is," Kintaro ventured. "Father would not lie . . ."

"Any man who refuses a child a stick of incense for his father's grave forfeits the right to call himself an uncle," Hiro said.

"But, if he's not, I have no family at all." Kintaro sniffed.

"Which merely means you have the opportunity to choose your own," Hiro replied. "Surely your parents were not blood relations?"

"No," Kintaro said.

"Yet they became a family."

"I can't get married," Kintaro said. "I'm still too little."

"Maybe so"—Hiro gestured to Father Mateo—"but you can find yourself a brother at any age."

He reached for the teapot. "Now, let's finish this before it gets too cold."

Later, as they left the teahouse, Kintaro asked, "Are you going to see my unc—the *washi*-maker who would not give me incense?"

"Can he tell us how the fires started?" Hiro asked.

Kintaro shook his head.

"Then why would we need to see him?"

Kintaro exhaled heavily in relief.

"I almost forgot to ask you," Hiro said. "Did you see Ishii-*san* do anything strange, either last night, or in the days before?"

"What do you mean by strange?" Kintaro asked. "Like being so afraid of fire he made us go to sleep when the sun went down? That's strange, and he did it every day."

"I was thinking more in terms of arguments," Hiro replied. "Or sneaking out when he thought you were asleep."

Kintaro shook his head. "He just made books. All day, every day. And then, at night, he snored."

"Would you like us to walk you back to Yuki's home?" Father Mateo asked.

"No, thank you. I know the way." Kintaro bowed. "Thank you very much for the tea and sweets."

"Thank you for showing us the teahouse," the Jesuit replied.

As the boy ran off into the maze of streets, Hiro started south along the sunny path that paralleled the river.

Father Mateo fell in step beside him. "And thank you for helping that poor child."

"I lied to him as well. We are going to talk with the washi merchant."

"Why?"

"The boy may not have set the fires, but I suspect he knows more than he's told us. I saw no point in pursuing the issue now—a child will cling to a lie like a dog to a bone. We will need more evidence to force the truth."

"What makes you think he lied?" Father Mateo asked. "And why do you think his uncle can help us prove it?"

Hiro stopped walking. "I meant what I said about that merchant forfeiting his right to be called an uncle. As to what he knows, or does not know . . . we'll learn those answers soon enough."

CHAPTER 21

As they continued down the path, Father Mateo asked, "Do you think there is a chance the fires might be related after all? What if the assassin who murdered Yasuari is working for someone who wants to drive the booksellers out of Edo, or to stop the guild from receiving recognition?"

"It seems more likely that the first two fires *were* accidents, and the assassin chose another book-related shop in the hope the authorities would not look too closely."

Father Mateo seemed confused, so Hiro continued, "The first two fires had obvious causes. A poppy smoker overturns a candle. Wood shavings ignite in a carver's shop. The guild had problems with fires in the past, and, given these recent issues, the assassin might have hoped the magistrate would blame this blaze on negligence too."

Father Mateo dropped his voice to a whisper. "Do you think the killer is one of Oda Nobunaga's spies?"

"Daisuke thinks so," Hiro said, "and the theory fits the facts, at least for now. However, the possibility remains that last night's fire was also just an accident. For example, caused by a boy who loves to read and fell asleep with a forbidden candle burning."

"Kintaro said he did not read last night, and that he only read by moonlight."

"He also described the fire in a way that suggests it began at the front of the shop—where he admits he was when the fire began."

"He was asleep."

Hiro gave the priest a knowing look. "Or so he claims."

"If he had been reading, he would have told us."

"Told us what? That he lit a candle in a place where his master expressly prohibited fire? That he, and not Ishii, was the one who broke a law for which the penalty is death?"

"No magistrate would execute a child." Father Mateo sounded deeply offended.

"The law makes no exceptions for children," Hiro said. "More importantly, an apprentice is not legally a child."

"I refuse to believe Kintaro was involved."

"We need to speak with the washi merchant either way." At the corner, Hiro turned right onto a narrow road lined with two-story buildings. Ahead in the distance, he could just see the watchtower of the fire brigade, rising above the tiled roofs. "But first, it's time for Yasuari to tell his tale."

"Yasuari is dead," the Jesuit said. "He cannot speak."

"By now, you should know he can," Hiro replied, "if you know how to listen."

Daisuke emerged from the fire watch tower as Hiro and Father Mateo approached.

"Good afternoon." He looked past them. "I admit, I am a bit surprised to see you here without Hiyoshi-*san*."

"He had something more important to attend to," Hiro said.

"Anything to do with the sign in Kawaguchi's window advertising fresh eels today?" Daisuke paused for only a moment before continuing, "I assume you have not come for an idle chat."

"We want to see the body from the fire." Although he saw no one nearby, Hiro decided not to voice Yasuari's name.

Daisuke gave a contemptuous laugh. "I thought I cured you of that urge many years ago."

Hiro fought the urge to clench his jaw, and did not reply.

"The corpse can teach you nothing," Daisuke said. "It's a waste of time."

"Nonetheless," Father Mateo replied, "it is our time to waste."

Daisuke seemed about to argue, but in the time it took to draw a breath, his expression changed. "Very well. I will take you to Komyō-ji."

The temple sat in a patch of forest at the edge of town. Frozen puddles lay on the ground beneath the trees, in the places sunlight never reached.

Daisuke led Hiro and Father Mateo through the two-story entry gate and down a gravel path between the trees. Incense smoke perfumed the air, combining with the scent of the pines to conjure memories of Hiro's childhood in the wilds of Iga. He banished the thoughts as quickly as they came. This was no time for reverie.

They reached the worship hall just as a bald-headed priest in a purple robe emerged, stepped into a pair of well-worn sandals, and descended the three wooden steps to the ground. When he reached the other men, he bowed.

Daisuke, Hiro, and Father Mateo returned the bow.

"Magistrate Hōjō asked these men to investigate last night's fire," Daisuke said. "They wish to see the body."

"We intend no disrespect," Father Mateo said.

"Of course." The priest bowed his head in assent. "Please come with me."

The three men followed the priest around the side of the worship hall and through the trees to a second, smaller hall. Its gently curving rafters paralleled the sweep of the branches on the massive pines. A narrow set of wooden stairs led up to a double set of sliding doors that formed the entrance. That afternoon, the doors stood open, allowing a view of the sacred space within.

At the back of the hall, a life-sized wooden Buddha sat in cross-legged meditation on a waist-high dais. The artist had carved the figure with its right hand raised to shoulder height, fingers extended to expose its palm in a gesture of peaceful blessing. The Buddha's heavy-lidded eyes looked downward, toward the place where the remains of Yasuari lay on a thin futon at the center of the hall.

The priests had arranged the pieces of the corpse as close to ana-tomically as possible. Delicate coils of scented smoke rose from an incense burner placed beside the dead man's head. The blackened blades of his swords lay at his side. Dark, ashy remnants littered the futon around the body, like rotting leaves at the base of a barren tree.

As Hiro ascended the steps and entered the hall, he noted the unmistakable odor of burned human flesh. Not even incense could erase the smell completely.

Father Mateo made the sign of the cross and bowed his head in silent prayer.

The Buddhist priest gave Daisuke an expectant look. When the fire commander nodded, the priest bowed deeply and left the hall.

Hiro knelt beside the corpse and tried to ignore the smell.

The corpse's skin looked taut and stretched. Bones protruded from the flesh, cracked badly by the fire's heat. Between the damage and the char, few useful details remained.

Father Mateo lowered his hands and raised his face, his prayer complete. "How long does it take a body to burn to ash?"

"It depends on the fire," Daisuke said, "but usually at least three hours. Four, to do the job completely."

"Have you any idea who killed this man? Or how?" Father Mateo asked.

"He was dead before the fire began," Daisuke said. "Beyond that? I cannot say."

"You are certain that he died before the fire?" the Jesuit pressed.

"His mouth is closed, and the body shows no sign of struggle. Any living man would have tried to escape the flames." Daisuke indicated the corpse's missing limbs. "More importantly, something cut his arms and legs off. Fires don't do that, and people don't survive it."

"You neglected to mention that detail to the magistrate," Father Mateo pointed out.

"He asked if limbs customarily burn off," Daisuke countered. "I answered honestly: sometimes, they do."

"And you think a bookbinder did this?" The Jesuit's tone suggested disbelief. "Overpowered and dismembered a trained shinobi?"

"An assassin did this," Daisuke corrected, "but yes, I think Ishii is that assassin. I asked him twice on the night of the fire if there was anyone else inside the shop. Both times, he claimed that he and his apprentice were alone."

"Perhaps he did not know the corpse was there," the Jesuit suggested. "After all, it makes no sense for him to burn his shop to hide a body. Waste and expense aside, he would have known the fire brigade would arrive before his victim burned to ash."

"The length of time it takes to burn a corpse is hardly common knowledge." Daisuke bent down and pointed to a place on the corpse's neck, where the skin had split in a horizontal line that paralleled the jaw. "And, for clarity, no one 'overpowered' Yasuari. The killer sneaked up from behind and slit his throat."

CHAPTER 22

"How do you know the killer was behind him?" Father Mateo asked.

Daisuke stared at the Jesuit. "Because only a fool would try to slit a man's throat from the front."

"I still don't think Ishii is guilty," the Jesuit insisted. "No artisan would set his own shop on fire."

"An artisan would not," Daisuke agreed, "but a shinobi would. Not only does it hide the corpse, or at least delay the identification, it also creates a perfect excuse to disappear. No one wonders why a man leaves town if his shop is gone, especially when he faces execution."

Hiro stood up. "This corpse has nothing more to teach us."

To his relief, Father Mateo did not argue.

"I told you so." Daisuke started toward the exit. "Maybe now you'll spend your time investigating things that actually might help us prove what happened to Yasuari."

"No one is stopping you from helping," Father Mateo said.

"Indeed, you seem quite eager to leave the difficult work to someone else," Hiro mused. "Perhaps I am not the one who has lost his edge."

Daisuke spun around. "Are you calling me afraid?"

"Merely observing facts, as I always do."

Daisuke glared at Hiro for the time it took to draw a breath.

Hiro returned the other shinobi's stare. He would not start a fight, but had no intention of backing down.

Unexpectedly, Daisuke turned away and left the hall.

Hiro and Father Mateo found the large man waiting by the temple gate. As they reached him, he fell in step beside the priest without a word.

Father Mateo opened his mouth to speak, but Hiro silenced him with a look.

When the three men returned to the fire watch tower, Daisuke asked, "Do you require any further aid this afternoon?"

"No," Father Mateo said, "but thank you for taking us to see the body."

Daisuke gave a noncommittal grunt and walked away.

"I hate to admit he was correct," Father Mateo said as Daisuke disappeared into the building at the base of the watchtower, "but I think that was a waste of time."

"We did confirm the cause of death," Hiro replied.

"You expect me to believe you did not see the gash in his neck at the fire scene?" Father Mateo asked. "I didn't see it, but it's not the kind of thing you would have missed."

"I saw it then as well," Hiro admitted, "but it did help to see the body one more time, to ensure that it had nothing more to tell us."

He set off toward Sora's shop. "Now it's time to see the washi maker."

The wooden shutters across the front of Sora's shop stood open, revealing the large display of books and manuscripts within. The works were arranged in a way that invited browsing, and a variety of colored woodblock prints hung on the walls and dangled from the rafters, all for sale.

Father Mateo gazed into the shop. "Is it normal for a single store to sell so many kinds of books and prints? Most of the merchants offer only a narrow range of items, and the artisans seem to specialize even more."

"The answer depends upon the shop," a female voice replied, "and, in this case, on my husband's generosity."

The speaker wore a midnight blue kimono and a silver obi shot with golden threads. She carried a bucket of water in her hands and a sleeping infant in a sling across her back.

Hiro guessed her identity at once. "Eiko-*san*?"

She bowed in acknowledgment. "Please forgive my presumption. Have you come with news of last night's fire?"

"What did you mean by your 'husband's generosity'?" Hiro asked.

Eiko nodded toward the shop. "My husband does not make decisions based on profit alone, as most men do. Ever since the other men elected him to lead the guild, he has felt an obligation to ensure the welfare of their businesses. He bought most of these works from other members of the *za* who required assistance."

"He purchased works that others could not sell?" Hiro asked.

"That, and from the shops of men who—"

"Need to sell for any other reason." Sora emerged from the room behind the shop and hurried toward them. "Do not let my wife's words fool you. I make quite a healthy profit on my wares."

Eiko bowed. "Forgive me. Now that my husband has arrived to help you, I should see to the evening meal." She started into the narrow passage between Sora's shop and the one next door.

"It was nice to meet you," Father Mateo called after her.

"Did you find Kintaro?" Sora asked.

"We did," Hiro replied. "Curiously, he mentioned having a relative in Edo."

Sora's smile faded. "An uncle—but they have no relationship."

"We would like to meet him anyway," Hiro said.

Sora hesitated. "Usaburo-*san* is a busy man—the head of the washi-makers' guild."

"I suspect that even a busy man can make time for an official investigation," Hiro said. "Where can we find him?"

"It may be easier if I take you there." Sora stepped out of the shop and into a pair of woven sandals that sat on a low stone shelf beside the storefront. As he stepped into the street, he called, "Ishii-*san*!"

The bookbinder emerged through the noren that separated the

shop from the rooms beyond. "You cal—oh! Good afternoon." The bookbinder bowed to Hiro and Father Mateo.

"I am taking them to see Usaburo-*san*," Sora explained. "Please watch the shop until I return."

At the end of the block, they turned onto a narrow street that curved sharply to the left, preventing them from seeing more than a couple of shops ahead. Two-story wooden buildings lined the road. The eaves of the upper stories overhung the lower floors just far enough to shelter the entrances, and a clean, pressed noren hung in every entry. Many of the buildings were connected to the ones next door, and shared a common wall. Raised lintels and decorative finials on the eaves showed where the roof of each shop ended and the next began.

The wooden planks on the facades were dark with age, but well-maintained. Even the street itself was clean, the frozen ground swept clear of all debris.

Men and women thronged the street, bowing and nodding politely to one another as they passed. Pedestrians moved to the sides of the road each time a group of laden porters or a horse-drawn cart passed by. The murmur of various conversations blended with the calls of merchants urging passersby to view their wares and the giggles of children playing in the road.

Hiro inhaled the mingled, ever-changing scents that filled the air: the salty tang of fish, the earthy musk of vegetables, and periodic wafts of fragrant incense from the shrines and temples scattered through the streets. He enjoyed the sights and smells, and felt no need to speak, but suspected Father Mateo's lower tolerance for silence would prompt the priest to start a conversation soon.

Within moments, the Jesuit proved him right. "Sora-*san*, you mentioned knowing young Kintaro all his life—did you know his father well?"

"Before he fell prey to the poppy's tears I considered him a friend. Kenji-*san* was the most talented calligrapher I have ever known. His skills surpassed what can be taught."

"It seems a pity that he could not train Kintaro," Father Mateo said, "and that the boy was forced to become an apprentice at such a tender age."

"Most regrettable," Sora agreed, "but I saw no feasible alternative. Kenji-*san* could not care for Kintaro properly. As the head of the za, I felt a duty to help Kintaro any way I could."

"Yet, his father's brother—Usaburo—felt no such duty?" Disapproval cut an edge in the Jesuit's question.

"Kenji-*san* and his brother had not been on speaking terms since long before Kintaro's birth," Sora explained. "Usaburo-*san* would not have helped the boy."

"Not even as a favor to the guild?" Father Mateo asked.

"That is a complicated question," Sora said. "You must understand, the washi guild has significant power. Thus far, it has helped to protect the artisans who use its wares, including those who create and sell books and scrolls. However, until my association becomes an officially sanctioned guild, I lack the ability to make a formal request for a favor or assistance—and even if I had that right, Usaburo-*sama* might well have refused it.

"His paper is the best in Edo but . . . regrettably, the same cannot be said of the man himself."

CHAPTER 23

U saburo's paper shop sat on a busy corner, three blocks from the river. The two-story building had more than twice the frontage of any other shop Hiro had seen in Edo. Elaborate ceramic finials in the shape of giant carp stood guard above the curving eaves, their tails curled above their heads as their sleepless eyes watched over the shop beneath. A cream-colored noren hung across the expansive entry, spotless but for the black, cursive kanji that coiled like a dragon down the side of the right-hand panel.

Father Mateo gestured to the characters. "Paper?"

"Usaburo-*sama*'s shop requires no other name," Sora replied.

Hiro parted the curtain and stepped inside. Overhead, a small bronze bell made a jingling sound, and continued to ring as Father Mateo and Sora followed him through the entrance.

Polished wooden planks covered the floor of the paper shop. Bronze fishing lanterns hung from the eaves, filling the room with golden light as bright as summer sun. On the far side of the shop, a second cream-colored noren hung in a doorway that led to unseen rooms beyond.

Wooden boxes, open at the front and stacked like shelves, lined every wall. Each opening held a different type of paper: folded, cut in sheets, or carefully rolled for use in scrolls, in a wide variety of weights and textures. Four long rows of waist-high tables, each with more shelves underneath, ran down the length of the shop from back to front. These, too, held many different types of paper.

Hiro felt himself relax as he inhaled the familiar, comforting scents of wood and expensive washi. The smell reminded him of the tiny room where he had spent many pleasant childhood hours watching his father draw or paint.

"What do you want?" the gruff demand pulled Hiro from his reverie.

The man to whom the voice belonged had just emerged through the noren at the back of the paper shop. He wore a spotted apron over striped hakama and a surcoat with the sleeves tied back, revealing muscular arms made strong by years of lifting heavy stacks of paper. The hair around his temples had gone silver, though the thick, dark tuft atop his head remained completely black.

Deep frown lines ringed the proprietor's mouth, and his lips turned down in the manner of a man who seldom smiled. He folded his arms across his chest. "It's not your day to purchase paper, Sora."

"Good afternoon, Usaburo-*sama*." Sora bowed. "These gentlemen have come to see—"

"This is a shop, not an exhibition," Usaburo said. "If you're not buying washi, move along."

Hiro felt an unexpected urge to make a purchase. *No man so unpleasant stays in business, much less leader of a guild, unless his wares are exceptional indeed.*

"Forgive the intrusion." Father Mateo bowed. "I am Fa—"

"I don't care if you're Dainichi Nyorai," Usaburo declared. "If you're not buying paper, go away. It's late in the day, and I am a busy man."

"Interesting." Father Mateo looked around. "In Kyoto, 'busy' implies that a shop has customers, and yet, I notice yours has none. I guess that word means something different here in Edo."

Hiro blinked in disbelief.

Usaburo gestured to the noren at the back of the shop. "I have a batch of paper draining, and half a dozen more to make today. My time is valuable, and you are wasting it."

"There was another fire last night—" Sora began.

"You think I have not heard?" Usaburo shook his head slowly. "Three fires in less than two months' time. Not good news for your little guild, Sora-*san*."

"These men have come on order of the magistrate," Sora persisted, though his tone made an apology of the words. "They wish to speak with you about . . . Kintaro."

"Is that miserable little beggar still alive?" Usaburo sneered. "I half expected you to say he froze to death, crying for incense in the street on the anniversary of his father's death."

Father Mateo gave the artisan a withering look. "Kintaro is your brother's son."

"On the contrary," Usaburo said, "dead men cannot sire children. My brother died to me the day he abandoned his duty to our family and this shop to become a *calligrapher*. I care nothing for the child he sired. Kenji made his choice."

"You cannot hold a child responsible for his father's choices," Father Mateo argued.

"I did not even know my worthless brother had a child until Sora asked if I would make him my apprentice." Usaburo snorted. "As if I would even consider such a thing."

Father Mateo turned to Sora. "You said . . ."

The guild leader's cheeks flushed red. "I said I could not speak to him formally. I still tried."

"You pulled me from my work to ask about my wastrel brother and his equally useless child?" Usaburo shook his head in disgust.

"That, and I require writing paper," Hiro said.

It was Father Mateo's turn to blink in disbelief.

"Now that, I can help you with." Usaburo looked down his nose at Hiro. "Although I should warn you: ronin normally can't afford my wares."

"In Kyoto," Hiro said, "merchants don't ask what samurai can afford."

Usaburo's right eye twitched at the insulting use of "merchant" over "artisan."

"Perhaps you had not noticed," Usaburo replied, "but you are no longer in Kyoto."

Hiro reached into the purse that hung from his obi and removed a silver coin.

"What are you doing?" Father Mateo demanded in Portuguese.

"Trust me," Hiro murmured back in kind.

Usaburo gave an approving nod at the sight of the coin. "It would appear Kyoto breeds a better class of ronin. Do you want plain washi, or something decorative?"

Hiro raised an eyebrow. "Do I look like the kind of man who needs decorative paper?"

"One never knows, with men from Kyoto." Usaburo lifted a single sheet from a nearby stack and turned to Hiro, holding the paper carefully by the corners. "My finest washi. How many sheets do you desire?"

Hiro returned the coin to his purse and held out his hand. "May I examine it more closely?"

Usaburo drew back reflexively. "Your hands are clean?"

"They will leave no marks on the page."

Usaburo relinquished the paper, but hovered over Hiro like a father watching a stranger handling his infant son.

The washi weighed almost nothing. Its textured surface felt sturdy and slightly rough. Tiny, dark brown flecks dotted the creamy surface at irregular intervals.

"I trust it meets your needs," Usaburo said.

Hiro handed the paper back to the artisan. "It would, if I were painting landscapes, but I asked for writing paper." Noting the question in Father Mateo's eyes, he added, "Any letter I wrote on that would blur beyond legibility."

Shifting his attention and words back to Usaburo, he added, "Moreover, if that is the finest washi you produce, I would like to speak with the man who made the rest of the pages in this shop."

Usaburo returned the paper to its place atop the pile. "I am persuaded. You are worthy of my time." He walked to the shelves on the far side of the shop and returned with another pale page, which he offered to Hiro. "Local fibers, mixed with white shell powder. Every sheet hand cut and aged three years. If you are competent with ink, I guarantee this will not run or bleed."

The paper felt smooth and slightly cool to the touch, with just enough weight and texture to feel expensive. Although not as skilled a calligrapher as his father or his younger brother Kazu, Hiro recognized the quality of the page. He handed the paper back. "Quite nice, but also not your finest."

"No," Usaburo agreed. "However, it is the grade you wanted."

"He did not mention a specific grade," Father Mateo said.

"He did not need to," Usaburo replied. "He is ronin, traveling in the company of a foreigner—which means he does not need the highest grade, or even the grade required for official documents. That said, he is clearly a literate man, well-versed in paper. By process of elimination, this"—he raised the sheet of paper in his hands—"is the grade he wanted."

And that is the reason your shop does well, when you have all the charm of a rotten squash, Hiro thought. Aloud, he said, "I will buy thirty sheets."

CHAPTER 24

"Do you wish to take the paper with you?" Usaburo asked. "If you prefer, I can also arrange delivery anywhere in Edo, at no charge."

"In that case, deliver it to the Kaeru Ryokan." Hiro handed the artisan a silver coin. "Before we go, do you know anything about the cause of the recent fires in Edo?"

"I understood the magistrate ruled them accidental." Usaburo looked suspicious. "Has new evidence come to light in the wake of last night's fire?"

"No," Sora answered. "Magistrate Hōjō simply asked these men to confirm his findings."

"Interesting." Usaburo returned his gaze to Hiro. "How long will your investigation run?"

"A week at most," Hiro replied.

"I will call a meeting of the washi guild and ask about this issue. If I learn anything of note, I will send word to you at the Kaeru Ryokan."

"We would be happy to attend the meeting," Father Mateo said.

Usaburo narrowed his eyes at the priest. "That would not be convenient."

"Thank you, but it's no trouble," the priest replied, "we are happy to make ourselves available on your schedule."

"It would not be convenient because I did not invite you to attend." Usaburo gestured to the door. "Now, our transaction is complete, and you may go."

"I apologize for Usaburo-*sama*," Sora said as he led Hiro and Father Mateo down the street away from the washi shop. "As the head of the most powerful guild in Edo, and a man who enjoys the daimyō's personal patronage . . ."

"You have no responsibility to explain his actions," Hiro said.

"But you do need to explain your own." Father Mateo sounded angry. "Buying paper, after the terrible things he said."

"It was the only way to get his cooperation," Hiro answered. "I've known plenty of men like him. They will not draw a breath to help a stranger, but a knowledgeable customer, they respect."

The Jesuit fell silent, although his expression clearly conveyed dissatisfaction.

As they turned the final corner and entered the block where Sora's bookshop stood, the guild leader finally broke the silence. "With apologies for my presumption, have you uncovered evidence connecting Kintaro with the fires? That is, beyond the known coincidences?"

"Nothing definite," Hiro replied.

"With respect, if you have no evidence, perhaps . . . at least, it seems to me that it would be more helpful to investigate the body in the fire."

"I could not agree with you more," Father Mateo said.

Just then, a panicked voice called, "Sora-*san*! You have returned!"

All three men looked toward the sound.

Ishii stood in the street, directly in front of Sora's shop. Hiyoshi stood behind him, securing a rope to the bookbinder's wrists.

"Sora-*san*!" Ishii repeated urgently, "I need your help!"

The guild master hurried toward the shop, with Hiro and Father Mateo right behind.

"What is happening?" Sora asked as he reached the storefront.

"Why did you leave this man unsupervised?" Hiyoshi demanded. "He left your shop. He was going to run away. I arrived just in time to stop him. But for me, he would be gone."

"I did not try to flee." Ishii nodded to a slender broom that lay on the ground at his feet. "I merely stepped outside to sweep the street."

"Your claims do not fool me," Hiyoshi said. "You are a slippery eel, but you will not escape! I realized, at lunch, that you would try to run—and I was correct! Sora-*san*, why did you leave this man alone?"

"I was not alone until you sent Sora-*san*'s wife away to find him," Ishii protested. "Eiko-*san* was here the entire time."

"Do not disrespect me!" Hiyoshi said. "I am samurai!"

"I am telling the truth. Why would I run away carrying a broom?" He looked down at his toes, which overhung the end of the light straw sandals on his feet. "These aren't even my shoes. They belong to Sora-*san*. I merely borrowed them to wear while I swept the street."

"And now you admit to theft as well!" Hiyoshi declared. "You see? You are a criminal!"

"Ishii-*san* has stolen nothing," Sora said, "and, with respect, I believe he speaks the truth."

"The magistrate confined him to the shop." Hiyoshi emphasized the final word. "That means he had to stay inside."

Sora started to object, but Hiro spoke over him. "Did your visit have any purpose other than to arrest Ishii?"

"I was looking for you," Hiyoshi said. "Daisuke-*sama* wants to see you."

"He sent you to find us?" Hiro found that difficult to believe.

Hiyoshi raised his chin. "He wants to see you as soon as possible."

"Then we have no time to waste on unnecessary arrests." Hiro indicated Ishii. "Sora-*san*, will you take responsibility for ensuring that this man does not escape?"

"I don't want to escape," Ishii repeated. "I only wanted to sweep the street."

Sora shot the bookbinder a warning look. "Of course. I will ensure he obeys the magistrate."

Hiro gestured to the rope that bound Ishii. "Release this man, and take us to Daisuke."

"He had better stay inside the shop," Hiyoshi warned as he removed the restraint. "If I see him outside unsupervised again, I will arrest him, no matter what you say."

CHAPTER 25

"Daisuke is waiting for us at the tower," Hiyoshi said as the structure came into view.

The wooden watchtower rose into the sky like an accusing finger, more than twice as tall as the two-story buildings on either side. Four shadowed figures stood on the sheltered platform at the top. Spreading eaves shadowed their features, but Hiro recognized Daisuke's bulky silhouette as the fire commander started down the narrow ladder that connected the platform to the ground.

Hiro, Father Mateo, and Hiyoshi reached the foot of the ladder at the same time as Daisuke.

The dōshin bowed. "I found them for you, Daisuke-*sama*."

Daisuke frowned. "I sent Ryuu to find them."

"I heard you tell him that you wished to see them," the dōshin explained, "and I knew that I could find them first. You see? I am a capable assistant."

Daisuke's disapproval deepened. "Did you tell Ryuu that you stole his task? Or merely leave him to search for them indefinitely, because he will not find them?"

"I had not thought of that," Hiyoshi said. "I merely wanted to prove that I could help."

"You merely wanted to stick your nose in matters that do not concern you," Daisuke retorted.

Hiyoshi crossed his arms. "Magistrate Hōjō said I could help."

Daisuke took a deep, slow breath, as if attempting not to lose his temper. "If you want to *help*, go find Ryuu and tell him he can return to the fire tower."

"At once, Commander!" Hiyoshi bowed and headed off at an eager pace.

Father Mateo watched him go. "You do not need to treat him so unkindly. He is trying to help."

"That man is a liability," Daisuke said. "The kind that gets people killed at a fire scene."

"He will not be your concern much longer." Hiro pointed out. "Why did you want to see us?"

Daisuke opened the door to the building at the base of the tower. "Let's talk inside."

The door opened onto a single, expansive room with an earthen floor at the front and a raised, tatami-covered platform at the back that served as a combination storage and sleeping area for the fire brigade.

Late afternoon sunlight angled through slatted windows on the west side of the building, painting the tatami and the floor with stripes of burnished gold. Dust motes danced in the beams.

A cluster of long, hooked staves stood upright in a pair of wide-mouthed barrels just to the left of the entry door. Beyond them, coiled ropes and other implements hung from pegs affixed to the wooden wall, above a pair of giant baskets like the ones Daisuke and Ryuu had carried to the fire. Hooks affixed to the right wall of the room held bamboo ladders, which were hung horizontally to keep them off the floor.

The earthen area at the front of the room was empty except for a knee-high stove of earth and clay, which sat alone at the center of the floor. That afternoon, the stove was dark and cold. The scents of ancient smoke and stale sweat perfumed the chilly air.

"Where is everyone?" Father Mateo asked as he stepped inside.

"I have three men in the tower, plus Ryuu." Daisuke waited for Hiro to enter the building and then closed the door behind them. "The rest of the men work different jobs during daylight hours. They will come if they hear the fire bell.

"I sent for you because my men discovered bones from Yasuari's other leg in the ashes at the fire scene. There are marks on the ends that appear to be made by a sword, or something similar, which confirms the body was dismembered." Daisuke looked grim. "That, in turn, confirms without question that he was dead before the fire began, most likely at the hand of a trained assassin."

"Then Ishii was not responsible after all." Father Mateo sounded vindicated.

"I fail to see how you reached that conclusion," Daisuke replied.

"Ishii-*san* had no reason to destroy his shop to hide a body that had been cut in pieces already," the priest explained. "He simply could have dropped them in the river."

"Simply." Daisuke made a dismissive sound. "Clearly, you have never tried to dispose of a dismembered body. Items dropped in rivers have an annoying habit of resurfacing along the bank, or getting caught on pilings. Also, people tend to notice someone carrying a body toward the river—more so, when that body is in pieces. A hand, or even a head, you might conceal, but a torso?" After a meaningful pause, he concluded, "This evidence proves the bookbinder is to blame."

When Father Mateo still looked unconvinced, Daisuke continued, "It fits the rest of the facts as well. Ishii moved to Edo a little over a year ago, and no one knows for certain where he came from. He lives alone, keeps to himself, and closes his shop unusually early every night—a perfect cover story for a man who wants to sneak out unnoticed."

"Put that way, it does require more investigation," the priest admitted.

"Fortunately, a detailed investigation is not required," Daisuke said. "The law already holds Ishii responsible for the fire. You need not risk exposing the Iga ryu—or yourselves—to danger by further investigation."

"But . . . what if he is not guilty?" Father Mateo asked. "We do not need to announce the evidence, if doing so would threaten the Iga ryu, but Hiro and I cannot condemn an innocent man to die."

Daisuke laughed without humor. "You, perhaps. Hattori Hiro has no trouble betraying the innocent."

Hiro stifled his irritation and kept his face a mask.

"Have you forgotten our conversation, Hiro-*san*?" Daisuke asked.

"I arranged for the magistrate to let you lead the investigation to ensure we could protect the ryu, obtain the information we require, and leave this town alive."

"I understand your"—Hiro stifled the urge to say *cowardice*—"urgent need to return to Iga, but you know as well as I that Hanzō will demand a better answer than 'it seemed apparent that he was a spy, and that seemed good enough.'"

"Then you had better find the answer quickly," Daisuke said, "and be careful how you go about it. Because you also know as well as I what a spy will do when he perceives a threat."

Long shadows filled the streets as Hiro and Father Mateo left the watchtower. When they had walked almost a block, the Jesuit asked, "What did Daisuke mean when he said you have no trouble betraying the innocent?"

"My past is a corpse we need not exhume, with fresher ones in need of our attention," Hiro answered.

Father Mateo frowned. "Do you believe Ishii-*san* is shinobi?"

"As you said, it merits further investigation. The fact that he owns a storehouse means most of his wealth escaped the fire, and the loss of the shop does give him a believable excuse to leave the city if someone else is punished for the fire."

"We should inspect the storehouse," Father Mateo said. "We might find evidence inside—shinobi tools, or weapons."

"Doubtful," Hiro answered. "He would want his weapons close at hand, and would not have let Kintaro take the books to the warehouse every night, unsupervised, if anything inside would have revealed his true identity. However, this new information also raises questions about the fire."

"I don't understand." Father Mateo stepped to the side of the road to allow a cart to pass.

Hiro switched to Portuguese as a shaggy, potbellied horse pulled the vehicle past, its owner walking slowly at its side. "Why would you bother dismembering a body if you planned to burn a building down around it?"

"I would not dismember a corpse under any circumstances," the priest replied. "But you make a valid point." He looked around. "This isn't the way to the ryokan."

"I want to make one final stop this evening," Hiro said. "To speak with someone that knows Ishii and has no apparent motive to tell a lie."

CHAPTER 26

Yuki sat on a wooden stool outside her door, with a basket of clean, white *tabi* on the ground beside her feet. She held a sock in one hand and a threaded needle in the other, but her hands lay idle. She looked upward, toward the sky, where the clouds glowed gold and orange in the light of the setting sun. The temperature had dropped to an uncomfortable level as the sun sank out of sight, but the woman seemed oblivious to the chill.

"Good evening, Yuki-*san*," Hiro said as he drew near.

She set the sock in the basket, stood, and bowed. "Good evening. I confess, I did not expect to see the two of you again. Kintaro is not here. He went to visit his father's grave." Her voice took on a hint of rebelliousness as she added, "I gave him coins to buy incense at the temple."

"We have not come to see Kintaro," Hiro said. "This time, we wish to speak with you."

"I do not know what I can tell you that another could not say in more detail, but I will help you if I can." She looked concerned. "Is Kintaro in trouble?"

"Why do you ask?" Hiro took care to keep the question light.

"It seems a logical deduction," she replied, "considering that you keep showing up and asking questions."

"You seem fond of the boy," Hiro observed. "Have you known him long?"

"I had not met him personally until today, but Sora-*san* has talked of him so often that I feel as if I've known him several years." She smiled wistfully. "I felt so relieved when Ishii-*san* agreed to take him in after the accident at Goro's."

"Relieved?" Hiro prompted.

She gave a gesture that bordered on a shrug. "My brother had asked Ishii-*san* to take an apprentice several times, but until that day he always said he preferred to work alone."

"Did Ishii-*san* know Kintaro before the fires?" Hiro asked.

"I doubt it, although I do not know." Yuki smiled. "Most men do not consult unmarried women about their personal affairs."

"Or married women either," Hiro quipped.

"True enough," Yuki replied.

"Did Ishii-*san* tell your brother why he liked to work alone?" Hiro asked.

"That, I do not know. Sora-*san* does not discuss business when Eiko-*san* and I are in the room. He expects us to remain in the other room, or take a walk outside, when he talks privately with members of the guild."

"Then how did you learn that Ishii-*san* refused an apprentice?" Hiro asked.

Yuki gave him a knowing smile. "Not all men regard women— unmarried or otherwise—as unworthy of consultation. Sora-*san* asks us to leave because our presence makes some men uncomfortable. However, he discusses many problematic issues with me privately. He understands that women see problems differently than men do, and understands the value of alternative perspectives. One of many reasons my brother is an effective leader."

"He considered Ishii's refusal to take an apprentice problematic?" Hiro asked.

"Somewhat," Yuki replied. "Ishii-*san* keeps mostly to himself. My brother considers it unhealthy for people to spend their lives alone." After a momentary pause, she asked, "Do you think it possible that Kintaro set the recent fires?"

"What makes you ask?" Hiro replied.

She made a vague gesture. "People talk. Usually it means nothing. However, I have heard it mentioned—more than once—that Kintaro has significant connections to each of the recent fires."

"A fact we noted," Father Mateo said.

"And one we are looking into," Hiro added.

"I suspected as much." Yuki's tone and face remained inscrutable. "In that case, I wish to offer a word of caution. You cannot hold the boy to an adult standard."

"Legally, an apprentice is considered an adult," Hiro replied.

"A ten-year-old child is not an adult, no matter what the law may claim," Yuki said, "and the adults around him have a duty to protect him, and not to convict him on the basis of circumstances beyond his control."

"I agree completely," Father Mateo said.

Hiro shifted the conversation to a more useful topic. "Did anyone have a grudge against Ishii-*san*, or against anyone in your brother's guild?"

"Ishii-*san* had no enemies and no debts. That much I know. Sora-*san* examined Ishii-*san* thoroughly when he applied to join the association a year ago. For professional reasons and . . ." She sighed. "My brother harbored hopes that Ishii-*san* might agree to marry me, despite my age and 'somewhat difficult character.'"

Hiro stifled a smile. "Are those your brother's words?"

"Not originally," she said, "although he does not dispute them. Nor do I, if 'somewhat difficult' is the proper term for a woman who prefers to live alone."

"It does not offend you to be called difficult?" Father Mateo asked.

"The loss of my independence would offend me," she replied. "Mere words cannot."

"I take it you did not like the idea of marrying Ishii-*san*," Hiro said.

"I liked it no less than the thought of marrying any man," Yuki replied, "and he does strike me as more responsible than most. That said, he is a difficult man to judge."

"Has he made any enemies in Edo?" Hiro asked. "Or been involved in any arguments or disputes?"

She thought for a moment before answering. "None to which I would apply those words. No man pleases everyone at every moment, and his reclusiveness may have caused some slight offense, but, on the whole, I do not think he has prompted any true enmity."

"And Goro-*san*?" Hiro asked. "Did he have enemies?"

"No one who would set his shop on fire," Yuki said at once, "and no one expressed surprise that a fire occurred. However, I do believe your question about enemies might have merit with regard to Ishii-*san*. Although I have no facts to support my opinion, and, as I said, I find it hard to believe he has caused offense, I also find it difficult to believe that last night's fire could have begun through Ishii-*san*'s negligence.

"He has not lived in Edo long, but Ishii-*san* has acquired a significant reputation, both for the quality of his work and for his oddly cautious nature. Few artisans take such care to protect their customers' manuscripts, and their shops, against floods and fires. My brother knows far more about these facts than I do, and could tell you more . . . although, most likely, you have talked with him already."

"We will speak with him again," Hiro said.

Father Mateo nodded almost deeply enough to constitute a bow. "We thank you for your time."

CHAPTER 27

"It occurs to me that Sora-*san* himself merits further investigation," Father Mateo said as he walked with Hiro through the narrow streets toward the Kaeru Ryokan. "He appears to be an honest merchant, but a man who acquires his inventory from those in need..."

"May be tempted to help the need arise," Hiro finished. "That thought occurred to me as well, but we must proceed with caution. In fact, that is one reason I did not ask Yuki more about her brother. I suspect Daisuke is correct, and that a spy killed Yasuari. If that spy is still in Edo, he—or she—may attack us also, when we get close to revealing the truth."

"Then how do we proceed?" Father Mateo asked. "We can hardly go door to door and ask to speak with Oda Nobunaga's spies."

"We do not even know, for certain, that the killer works for Oda," Hiro said.

"Given our purpose here, you must admit it is the most reasonable answer."

"The most reasonable *assumption*," Hiro corrected. "Although I will acknowledge that, at the moment, it also seems like the most likely theory."

Hiro and Father Mateo returned to the ryokan to find Kaeru standing on the veranda, staring down the street.

Above her head, the roof tiles glowed with the last, reflected rays of the setting sun.

"Good evening," Father Mateo said.

"Good evening." Kaeru bowed.

Hiro followed her gaze back up the street, but saw only a few late travelers on the road. "Are you expecting someone?"

"Natsu-*san*." Concern etched lines in Kaeru's brow. "I hoped, perhaps, she might return tonight."

"Have you a reason to expect her?" Hiro asked.

"No, and no true reason to worry either." Kaeru drew her gaze away from the street. "But I know you plan to await her return, and do not wish to delay you any longer than required. Also, in truth, I must admit, after hearing your warning . . ." She shook her head. "Please ignore me. It is merely an unreasonable concern."

"On the contrary," Father Mateo said. "It seems entirely reasonable to me."

She smiled gratefully. "Are you hungry? The evening meal should be ready. I will bring it to your room at once—and please forgive my concerns about Natsu-*san*." She gave a rueful laugh. "Old women worry when there is no need."

Hiro and Father Mateo went inside, removed their sandals, and climbed the narrow stairs to the second floor.

As he opened the door to the guest room, Hiro noted the tube-shaped roll of washi sitting on the table.

It reminded him that, sooner or later, he would have to send a letter to Hattori Hanzō, explaining his decision to disobey orders, take over the assignment Hanzō intended for a different Iga agent, and come to Edo instead of taking Father Mateo to the Portuguese colony as instructed.

Given the events of the past few months, Hiro felt justified in his decisions.

Whether Hanzō would agree remained to be seen.

The stairs creaked as Hiro and Father Mateo knelt on opposite sides of the table.

A moment later, Kaeru arrived in the doorway, holding a heavily laden tray. Ana stood behind her, similarly burdened.

"May we enter?" Kaeru asked.

"Of course." Hiro lifted the paper from the table and set it carefully atop the nearby pile of quilts.

The savory scents of fish and broth that wafted from the dinner trays set Hiro's mouth to watering once more. He had eaten so much terrible food on the travel road that he felt a surge of gratitude for every well-cooked meal.

Kaeru set her tray on the table and stepped aside so Ana could do the same. As the housekeeper left the room, the innkeeper said, "Again, I apologize for bothering you with my concerns about Natsu-*san*."

"You have no need to apologize," Father Mateo said. "We understand."

"Thank you." Kaeru paused in the doorway. "If you wish more rice or tea, please let me know."

She stepped over the threshold and closed the door behind her.

Father Mateo bent his head in a silent blessing as the stairs squeaked their objection to the women's descent.

Hiro surveyed his dinner tray. Paper-thin slices of fresh *sashimi* rested on delicate, palm-sized dishes glazed the color of autumn leaves. Nearby, a pair of whole grilled fish sat side by side on a rectangular, black-glazed plate. Coils of pale, fragrant steam rose from the covered soup bowl and the heaping bowl of rice on the far-right side of the lacquered tray. Beside the rice, two tiny plates of bite-sized *tsukemono* rounded out the meal. To Hiro's delight, the pickled vegetables looked homemade.

Father Mateo said, "Amen," and reached for his chopsticks.

Hiro murmured "*Itadakimasu*," and began to eat. He savored every bite, from the tender sashimi that tasted of the deep, clean sea to the hearty soup of fresh root vegetables and tofu swimming in earthy broth. He refused to allow his concerns about Yasuari's death, or the possibility of enemy spies in Edo, prevent him from enjoying the evening meal.

Several minutes later, Father Mateo set his empty soup bowl down with a happy sigh. "Father Vilela says Edo has far to come before it rivals Kyoto, but food like this suggests it's not that far behind."

"It takes more than food to make a city prosper," Hiro said, "though Hanzō also believes, in time, Edo will rival Kyoto in importance. Personally, I doubt it."

Father Mateo rested his hands in his lap. "I suppose we should discuss the investigation."

"Have you had any new ideas?" Hiro asked.

"At some point, you should share *your* theories first," the priest replied, "although, I must admit, that thought does not precisely count as 'new.'"

"I keep returning to your comment that it makes no sense to dismember a body if you plan to burn the building down around it," Father Mateo continued. "Daisuke-*san* seems convinced that Ishii-*san* murdered Yasuari and set fire to the shop to hide the crime, but if the two events are not related . . . we definitely need to investigate other possibilities more closely, starting with Sora-*san*."

"Because he leads the guild?" Hiro asked.

"Among other reasons. For example, do you remember him interrupting Eiko-*san* before she could explain where he bought his inventory? In retrospect, it seems quite out of character for a man who cares about women's opinions as much as Yuki-*san* implied."

"You think the master of the booksellers' guild sets book-related shops on fire in order to buy the books that survive the flames?" Hiro asked.

"Put that way, it does seem foolish," the priest admitted. "In my head, it sounded far more reasonable."

CHAPTER 28

"It is reasonable," Hiro said, "and did occur to me as well, although we have no specific evidence to support it."

"It's an unreliable way to acquire inventory," Father Mateo pointed out. "Most of the time, the flames would destroy the books."

"Not if the artisans owned storehouses, as Ishii did," Hiro countered. "As guild leader, Sora-*san* would know who had one."

"In which case, the fire at Ishii's shop could have accidentally revealed a corpse the killer planned to dispose of elsewhere," Father Mateo said.

"Which still suggests Ishii is both a killer and a spy." After a moment's thought, Hiro continued, "As Daisuke mentioned, his behavior fits an assassin's profile. He has not lived in Edo long, comes from a place he has not disclosed, and seems to have no wife or family. He excels in his profession, but keeps to himself."

"In that case," Father Mateo mused, "why did he agree to take Kintaro as his apprentice? Especially since he refused Sora's requests to take an apprentice in the past."

"This time, the request was different," Hiro pointed out. "There was an urgent need. Such a request would be more difficult to refuse."

"Perhaps," Father Mateo said, "but why would he risk a murder, and cutting up a corpse, with Kintaro in the shop?"

"We do not know the murder happened in the shop," Hiro replied, "and, despite Daisuke's statements to the contrary, dismembered bodies aren't that difficult to move or hide, for someone with the proper skills."

"Even so, it must have happened recently," Father Mateo said. "Dead bodies stink within a day or two."

"It takes longer if you keep them cold—or submerged in water."

"Submerged . . ." Father Mateo looked confused, but only for a moment. "You think Ishii hid the corpse in the fire barrels? The ones he kept in the shop, in case of fire?"

"It would explain why no one saw the body, and might explain why the corpse was dismembered—to fit inside the barrel. Kintaro mentioned the lid would not come off when he tried to get inside. Perhaps the lid was more than merely 'stuck.'"

"But, in that case, wouldn't the body have shown evidence of immersion? Bloating, or . . . boiling?"

"Perhaps," Hiro acknowledged. "Regrettably, I have not seen enough bodies that were boiled and then burned to know what evidence to look for in such cases."

"Daisuke-*san* might know," the priest suggested.

"Which would require consulting him, as well as trusting him to tell the truth."

Father Mateo gave Hiro a searching look. "Why do you still judge him by his childhood acts? A man can change."

"Most men do not."

"Do you consider Daisuke-*san* a suspect?" Father Mateo asked.

Hiro began to answer *I don't know* but closed his mouth, the words unspoken. Eventually, he said, "I have no doubt that he would kill me, given cause, but I admit we have no evidence suggesting his involvement in this matter."

"That was quite a complicated 'no.'" Father Mateo gave the shinobi an earnest look. "You must forgive him for his childhood trespasses. This grudge harms only you."

"If I had not forgiven Daisuke, he would not be breathing." Hiro crossed his arms. "The fact that I don't like him does not mean I hold a grudge."

"Trust me," Father Mateo said, "you hold a grudge."

Hiro clenched his jaw and looked away, almost as frustrated by his own behavior as he was at the Jesuit for being right.

"How can we prove whether or not Ishii is an assassin?" Father Mateo asked. "And whether Sora sets fire to other men's shops to fill his own?"

Hiro uncrossed his arms at the conciliatory change of subject. "I have a few ideas, but nothing definite." He stood up. "I think I'll take a walk and think it through."

"Alone?"

Hiro gestured to the Jesuit's Bible, which lay on a cushion beside the table. "Unless you plan to skip your evening prayers."

"We could go afterward. I see no need for you to go alone."

"I can think of three." Hiro raised a new finger as he named each one. "The weather gets colder as it gets late, I think better in silence, and I can defend myself more effectively if I don't have to worry about you."

Father Mateo raised a hand toward his hair, but caught himself and lowered it to his side. "Whoever murdered Yasuari knows how to surprise and kill shinobi."

"True enough," Hiro replied, "but I have an advantage Yasuari may have lacked."

"Which is?"

Hiro smiled. "I am aware that someone wants to kill me."

"I do not find that reassuring." Dismay came over the Jesuit's face. "Are you doing this on purpose, to draw the killer out?"

"On the contrary, I do not believe that he—or she—would attempt an ambush while I am alone. Not as long as you remain alive to alert the authorities, anyway."

"An assumption," Father Mateo said, "and a dangerous one, at that."

"All assumptions are dangerous, if you rely upon them." Hiro started toward the door. "But I do not."

Hiro left the ryokan and wandered through the darkened streets. The night was still, and the air was cold. He raised the hood on his traveling cloak to warm his ears.

Golden light seeped through the shuttered windows of homes and shops, creating streaks and pools of light on the packed earth road. Here and there, a lantern twinkled like a giant star.

Overhead, the real stars twinkled in a moonless sky.

The few people Hiro passed wore heavy clothes and wasted no breath on conversation. They hurried through the streets at deliberate speed, as if intent on reaching the warmth of shelter.

Eventually, he found himself approaching the place where Kenji's calligraphy shop once stood. He had passed it earlier in the day, with Hiyoshi and Father Mateo, but the dōshin had hurried them past, claiming the empty space had no secrets to reveal. Indeed, the narrow lot had been thoroughly cleaned and swept, leaving no trace of the tragic fire except for a few streaks of smoke on the walls of the adjacent shops.

Hiro surveyed the empty space and thought about the events that happened there.

Nothing about the fire that killed Kintaro's father seemed suspicious. The effects of poppy tears could make even the most responsible people careless. Smokers often knocked things over in their stupor, and might not awake in time to escape a fire. Although he did not know if Kenji owned a storehouse, it seemed unlikely. A man who sold the book he made for his son most likely owned nothing else of value.

Most importantly of all, the facts surrounding the fire suggested that no one gained from Kenji's death, which made murder far less likely.

With a last, long look at the empty space, Hiro continued down the road.

As he walked toward the location of Goro's shop, it occurred to him that the fire that killed Kintaro's father could have inspired someone to set the second blaze. The hazardous state of Goro's shop created larger risks than just the danger to the artisan himself: the daimyō would not recognize a guild that presented a danger to the town. Setting the shop on fire was dangerous also, but the guild—and, by extension, Sora—absolutely gained from its destruction.

In fact, the guild leader would profit twice, if he also purchased Goro's inventory.

Hiro barely slowed as he passed the site of the second fire. He now knew what he had to learn, and this location would not hold the answers.

The more he considered Yasuari's murder, and the condition of the corpse, the more likely it seemed that the death was unrelated to the fire at Ishii's shop. The coincidental timing of the two events was strange, but even so, the evidence fit together best if the two events had separate explanations.

Unfortunately, when the events were viewed from that perspective, Kintaro returned to the fire suspect list—especially if Goro had no storehouse. Father Mateo would disagree, but Hiro would deal with that issue when it arose.

He slowed his pace as he approached the ruins of Ishii's home and shop.

A large stone lantern glowed in front of the neighboring building, casting a puddle of orange light in the darkened street. Its light illuminated the fire site just enough for Hiro to make out the pile of blackened rubble at the center of the lot.

He wondered if this site still had any secrets to reveal.

On the far side of the rubble, a shadow moved, and asked, "What are you doing here?"

As Daisuke moved into the light, Hiro thought, *I could ask the same of you.*

CHAPTER 29

Daisuke walked around the fire site toward Hiro.

As he watched the larger man approach, Hiro felt a surge of distrust and loathing. Despite the Jesuit's words to the contrary, Hiro doubted Daisuke would ever change. A child who bullied others once he reached the age to understand the consequences of that choice would grow into a man who abused his power.

Hiro had no use for such behavior, or the people who engaged in it.

Daisuke wore a heavy padded coat and pants so dark they disappeared into the shadows. He bowed to Hiro, who returned the gesture.

"What are you doing out at this time of night?" Daisuke repeated.

"Walking," Hiro said.

"Have you persuaded the foreigner to accept the law, and let the bookbinder take the blame?" Daisuke asked.

"You seem unusually eager for that outcome," Hiro said. "Should I wonder why? Or what you happen to be doing out in dark clothing at this time of night?"

"What are you insinuating?" Daisuke's voice acquired a hostile edge.

"You tell me."

Daisuke gestured in the general direction of the watchtower. "I was out on a patrol when I saw you coming. The tower's good for spotting larger fires, but many hazards become more apparent at eye level."

"I suppose you would know."

Daisuke narrowed his eyes. "I find your arrogance offensive."

Hiro recognized the words as an invitation to a fight.

Before he decided how to respond, a female voice called, "Matsui-san? Is that you?"

Hiro turned to see Yuki hurrying toward him.

"We will continue this conversation later," Daisuke murmured.

Yuki paused just long enough to bow before continuing, "Kintaro is missing. He did not return for the evening meal. I cannot find him anywhere."

"Have you checked with Sora-*san*?" Hiro asked.

"My brother has not seen him. No one has. For hours." Her voice was calm, but her eyes revealed worry.

"He probably lost track of time," Daisuke said. "Boys often do."

"Kintaro gave me his word that he would return by dark," Yuki replied.

Daisuke laughed. "I can think of few things less reliable than the word of a young boy."

Yuki stared at him for a moment and then shifted her gaze to Hiro. "Matsui-*san*, I have searched everywhere that I can think of. Will you help me look for him?"

"Go home," Daisuke said. "More likely than not, he's waiting for you there, outside the door. If you'll excuse me, I need to finish my patrol."

"Please watch for Kintaro as you go," Yuki called after him.

Daisuke disappeared into the darkness, giving no indication he had heard her.

"Matsui-*san*?" Yuki asked hopefully.

"I will help you. Tell me where you've searched."

Two hours later, Hiro returned to the ryokan to find Father Mateo shivering on the veranda. The Jesuit wore his traveling cloak and carried a lantern.

"What are you doing?" Hiro asked.

"Heading out to look for you." The Jesuit's expression hovered somewhere between rage and tears. "I wanted to leave an hour ago, but

Kaeru persuaded me to wait. She said you could take care of yourself, but even so, I thought . . ." He shook his head mutely.

Hiro understood. "I apologize. Let's go inside. I will explain why I was delayed."

As they entered the ryokan, a door beside the stairs slid open and Ana emerged with Gato in her arms. The cat gave a chirping trill at the sight of Hiro, although Ana's face was anything but pleased. "Hm. Where have you been?"

"Out for a walk." Hiro stroked Gato's head. She leaned into his hand with a happy purr. "The hour is late. We all should go to sleep."

"Next time, don't stay out so late." Ana retreated to her room. As the door slid shut behind her, Hiro heard her mutter something unintelligible under her breath.

Father Mateo started up the stairs without a word.

When they reached their room, the Jesuit shed his traveling cloak, knelt on his futon, and wrapped himself in a quilt against the cold. He barely gave Hiro time to shut the sliding door before he said, "Ana may have chosen not to argue, but I'm not sleeping until I hear what happened. And don't say it was a walk. Nobody walks for three hours in the cold."

Hiro knelt across from the priest and explained about the missing boy.

Father Mateo's frown dissolved, replaced by deep concern. "Did you find him?"

"Regrettably, no, and he had not returned to Yuki's home when I left her there a few minutes ago."

"Something happened to him," Father Mateo said. "He would not run away."

"He might have." Hiro paused. "If he was responsible for the recent fires."

"Kintaro would not set his father's shop on fire!" the priest declared.

"I was referring to the last two fires," Hiro said. "The one at Goro's shop, and at Ishii's."

"That boy did not burn down those shops." The quilt slipped off Father Mateo's shoulders as he crossed his arms. "I refuse to believe it, and I find your theory offensive."

"That opinion seems quite popular this evening," Hiro said. "And, to be clear, I did not say I believed Kintaro set the fires. I simply suggested that his disappearance seems suspicious, taking all of the circumstances into account."

"On that, we agree. In the morning, we are going to search until we find him."

Hiro felt a surge of relief. "I half expected you to insist that we continue the search tonight."

"I did consider it," the priest replied, "but if you and Yuki could not find him, I doubt you and I could do any better in the dark. We simply have to hope that he survives until tomorrow morning."

"Or that he returns to Yuki's home by then. He might, you know." Hiro tried to sound persuasive, but could tell the priest did not believe the words any more than Hiro did himself.

CHAPTER 30

The following morning, Father Mateo wanted to skip the morning meal and start the search at once.

Hiro thought of Kaeru's homemade tofu, miso soup, and rice. "We can search longer, and more effectively, with something in our stomachs."

"While Kintaro has nothing in his own," the Jesuit countered.

"You don't know that," Hiro answered. "We can hurry, but we need to eat."

Fortunately, the meal arrived at that very moment, and Father Mateo did not force the issue. However, the priest flew through his food so quickly that Hiro had to rush to match his pace.

As they finished the last of their soup and rice, Kaeru returned to the room. "I apologize for the intrusion," she said, "but I heard you mention a need to hurry. Has something happened?"

"We have a missing child to find." Father Mateo explained about Kintaro's disappearance, ending with, "I fear for his safety. He had no reason to run away."

"Are you certain?" Kaeru gave Hiro a meaningful glance.

"Have you heard something?" Father Mateo asked.

"Nothing definite." Kaeru bent and retrieved the tray of empty dishes. "On second thought, it was probably not worth mentioning."

"But you did mention it," the Jesuit said, "so please, continue."

"Most likely, it's unfounded gossip, but I heard a rumor that the boy was responsible for the recent fires."

"When and where did you hear this?" Father Mateo asked.

"Yesterday afternoon, at the apothecary. She was talking with someone about the boy buying camphor paste shortly before the fires." Kaeru looked at Hiro. "Knowing who your mother is, I doubt I need to explain the significance of that to you."

"What were you doing at the apothecary?" Hiro asked.

"I needed willow bark, to treat a headache." Kaeru said. "If you wish to speak with Bin-*san*, you can find her shop in the block to the south of the building that burned down two nights ago."

"The apothecary is a woman?" Father Mateo asked.

"She ran the shop with her husband, until he died two years ago," Kaeru replied. "Since then, she runs it on her own."

"And people trust her?" Father Mateo flushed. "I apologize. I did not mean to imply . . . that is, I merely meant that men—well, *some* men . . ." He gave up, too flustered to continue.

"Bin-*san* and her shop do fine without such men," Kaeru said.

"Is this apothecary one of us?" Hiro asked.

"No. Merely an elderly woman with a lifetime of experience. Her husband trained with Dōsan, in Kyoto, and taught Bin-*san* everything he learned. Her skills as a healer rival even your mother's."

"Did you know my mother well, when you lived in Iga?" Hiro asked.

"No," Kaeru admitted, "but Natsu did. Your mother trained her."

"Do you think Bin-*san* will tell us about Kintaro?" Father Mateo asked.

"There may be nothing of consequence to tell," Kaeru said, "but I think it would not hurt to ask."

As the door slid closed behind her, Father Mateo said, "Hiro, we should see the apothecary before we start our search. If she has useful information, hearing it is worth a short delay."

Despite Kaeru's instructions, Hiro and Father Mateo almost walked right past the apothecary's tiny shop. The storefront measured barely longer than a noodle vendor's cart, and consisted of a single wooden panel and a narrow door. A noren hung in the entry, indicating the shop had opened for the day.

"This can't be the place," Father Mateo said as they reached the entrance. "Kaeru indicated the shop was prosperous."

"Perhaps the owner doesn't want to pay the higher taxes for more frontage." Hiro parted the dark blue noren and stepped inside.

The interior of the shop was several times as long as it was wide. A tiny shoe rack sat inside the door, in a small, square entry that opened directly onto the wood-floored shop. A waist-high wooden counter separated the right side of the shop, where customers could sit or stand, from the rows of floor to ceiling shelves along the left-hand wall, which held the apothecary's wares.

Ceramic bottles, jugs, and jars marched down the shelves in perfect rows, each one precisely placed and equidistant from the ones on either side. A few of the containers had colorful glazes and painted patterns, but most had no adornment other than the Chinese characters that described their contents, brushed down the side of the jars in a spidery hand.

Three wooden stools sat in front of the counter, giving customers a place to sit while waiting their turns to see the apothecary. At the moment, however, all of the stools—like the shop itself—were empty.

A second noren hung across a narrow doorway at the far end of the shop.

Hiro and Father Mateo waited, but no shopkeeper appeared.

Eventually the Jesuit called, "Good morning . . . is the apothecary here?"

"Yes, yes, I'm coming," a female voice replied.

The noren at the back of the shop parted to reveal a woman who moved with a speed and vigor that belied her bony frame and snow-white hair. She paused at the sight of Father Mateo.

"Well. This is a first."

She bowed politely before continuing down the narrow aisle on the left side of the shop, walking between the shelves and the wooden counter until she stood directly opposite the priest. "I don't believe a foreigner has ever come into my shop before. I am Bin, the apothecary. How may I help you?"

Hiro turned to the priest. "Show her your hands."

Reflexively, Father Mateo drew his hands to his body and covered his scarred left hand with his right one. "Why?"

"They pain him in cold weather," Hiro said to Bin, "the left one in particular."

"How did you know?" Father Mateo asked.

"You rub the joints. Did you think I did not notice?"

Bin made an expectant gesture. "Show me."

Slowly, Father Mateo unclenched his hands and rested them on the counter.

The apothecary regarded them thoughtfully. "How did you get these scars?"

"A dog attacked me," Father Mateo said.

"It attacked his housekeeper," Hiro corrected. "He jumped between them and took the injury on her behalf."

"You stepped between a Japanese woman and a dog?" Bin frowned at the Jesuit's hands. "A large dog, by the look of it." She nodded. "I can help with this."

"I have heard that camphor paste is good for aches," Hiro commented.

Bin's expression transformed in an instant. She narrowed her eyes and backed away from the counter. "It appears I was mistaken. I cannot help the foreigner. You should go."

CHAPTER 31

Father Mateo removed his hands from the counter. "With apologies . . . I do not understand."

Bin ignored him and spoke to Hiro. "The fact that his injuries are clearly real makes your deception even more repugnant."

"We made no attempt to deceive you," the priest objected.

"You are the foreigner and the samurai appointed by the magistrate to investigate the recent fires," Bin declared. "Do not deny it—and do not try to deny that Sora sent you, either. I spoke with him honestly—despite the ethical issues involved in discussing my customers' private business—because I trusted him to keep his word, but I cannot afford to acquire a reputation for indiscretion. I have nothing more to say to you."

"Sora-*san* did not send us," Hiro said.

Bin regarded him silently.

"We were given your name by Kaeru-*san*, the innkeeper." Hiro made a calculated guess. "She heard you talking with Sora-*san*."

Bin's expression softened a fraction. "Kaeru-*san*?" Slowly, understanding spread across her wrinkled face. "I did not realize she had overheard."

"Young Kintaro has disappeared," Father Mateo said. "If you have any information that explains what happened, or can help us find him . . . . Please, we need your help."

"Just a moment." Bin walked around the end of the counter, removed a wooden sign from a peg beside the entrance to the shop, and disappeared into the street.

A moment later she reappeared and closed the wooden door behind the noren. As she slid a wooden lever into place to secure the door, she said, "I will tell you what I know, because I trust Kaeru-*san*."

She returned to her customary place on the far side of the wooden counter. "Sora-*san* came to see me yesterday afternoon, asking about customers who purchased camphor paste from me recently. When I told him I could not share that information, he asked whether I would confirm—confidentially—whether any of the men whose shops burned down bought camphor paste."

"To which you said?" Father Mateo prompted.

"That apothecaries do not tell tales about our customers. I also told him that half the artisans in Edo use camphor paste, either as a treatment for painful joints or as a pest repellant. Kaeru-*san* buys it regularly, too.

"It is not dangerous, so long as you keep it away from open flame.

"However, it is also true that two of the men whose shops burned down bought camphor from me shortly before the fires. Kenji-*san*—Kintaro's father—had not purchased anything from me for several months. The day I refused to sell him poppy tears, he said he would never darken my door again, and he kept his word."

"You refused to sell him poppy tears?" Father Mateo repeated.

"I will not sell a remedy that does more harm than good." She paused. "Are you aware of the hunger poppy tears can cause if smoked too often?"

Hiro nodded.

"I do sell them"—she made a general gesture toward the shelves behind her—"but only in cases of urgent need. When Sora-*san* told the apothecaries' guild that Kenji had the hunger, we agreed we would not sell to him anymore."

"But someone did," Hiro said.

Her face looked grim. "I do not know who."

"Did you sell poppy tears to anyone in the last few weeks before Kenji died?" It was a long shot, but Hiro asked the question anyway.

Bin thought for a moment. "A woman bought some for her husband—a hunter, who was gored by a boar."

"A boar?" Father Mateo asked.

"They are dangerous in winter, and worse in spring, when the babies come," Bin said. "That was my only sale of poppy tears this winter."

"Do you know Kintaro well?" Hiro asked.

Bin rested her hands on the counter and said nothing. Eventually, she sighed. "Sora-*san* told you all about it, didn't he?"

"We would prefer to hear the truth from you directly," Hiro bluffed.

She looked defeated. "I suppose there is no harm in repeating what Sora-*san* already told you. Ishii-*san* made his recent purchase of camphor paste himself, but Goro-*san* did not. Kintaro bought it for him, on the afternoon before the fire destroyed Goro-*san*'s shop."

"Kintaro bought camphor paste?" Hiro asked.

"When I asked, he told me Goro-*san* had sent him," Bin replied. "I questioned him quite thoroughly, because Goro-*san* had purchased a large pot of camphor paste the week before. Kintaro claimed his master dropped the other pot accidentally, and ruined it in the dirt."

"But now you wonder . . ." Hiro trailed off, hoping the woman would complete the thought.

"On the contrary," Bin said firmly. "At the time, I believed he told the truth, and I still believe it. You would understand, had you known Goro-*san*."

Father Mateo rubbed the back of his left hand with the fingers of the right. "Did Sora-*san* mention why he asked about the purchases in the first place?"

"I should think that obvious," Bin replied. "He is afraid the recent fires were not accidents after all."

"Did he say so directly?" Hiro asked.

"He said he was searching for information that might help your investigation. In particular, information about Kintaro. To be clear: I do not share or agree with his concerns."

"Did the boy make other purchases?" Hiro asked. "Or just the camphor?"

"He had never purchased anything from me before, and purchased nothing else," Bin answered. "However, I had seen him before that day, because he came in with his father several times, before Kenji succumbed to the lure of poppy tears."

"Can you tell us anything else about the recent fires?" Hiro asked.

"Or why Kintaro might have run away?" Father Mateo asked. "Especially since you do not think he used the camphor paste to set the fires."

"I have told you everything I know," Bin said. "There is no more."

"We appreciate you speaking with us," Father Mateo said.

The apothecary reached beneath the counter and withdrew a palm-sized ceramic pot. "Please take this, with my apologies."

Father Mateo accepted the pot and raised the tiny lid.

The familiar, astringent scent of camphor paste made Hiro's eyes begin to water.

"Your friend is correct"—Bin nodded to Hiro—"it is the most effective treatment for your hands. Rub just a touch into the joints each time they hurt."

Father Mateo replaced the lid on the pot and tucked it carefully into a fold of his obi. "Thank you very much—for everything."

The two men left the apothecary's shop and walked along the edge of the hard-packed street, leaving room for the carts and porters that already clogged the narrow road.

"Where should we begin the search for Kintaro?" Father Mateo asked.

"By confirming whether or not he is still missing," Hiro answered.

"Then we need to go that way." Father Mateo pointed in the direction of Yuki's home.

Hiro did not change direction. "We have one brief stop to make along the way."

CHAPTER 32

Sora had just begun to open the wooden shutters at the front of his shop as Hiro and Father Mateo approached the storefront.

The guild leader stopped and bowed. "Good morning. Have you news?"

Hiro looked past Sora. "Are you here alone?"

Worry flashed in the guild leader's eyes. "Ishii-*san* is here, but he is sleeping. Can this matter wait until he wakes?"

"He is still sleeping at this hour?" Hiro found that strange.

Sora glanced over his shoulder and then lowered his voice. "He did not sleep well last night. I woke up several times, myself. Each time I heard him pacing, back and forth, across his room. If it is possible to let him sleep, it would be kind."

"As it happens, it is you I wish to speak with," Hiro said. "About Kintaro."

"Has the boy done something wrong?"

"You tell me," Hiro replied.

Sora looked away. "I don't know what you mean."

"You can start with the concerns you expressed to Apothecary Bin."

A guilty expression appeared on Sora's face. "I apologize, I should have told you. I went to see her yesterday afternoon, after I learned that you suspected Kintaro's involvement in the fires. You see . . . the day after Goro's execution, I heard a rumor that the boy was seen carrying a pot of camphor paste the afternoon before the fire broke out, and that he yelled at Goro-*san* and ran away from the shop shortly before the fire occurred. At the time, I thought the story was entirely untrue. But yesterday afternoon, after I went with you to see Usaburo-*sama*, my sister confirmed that Kintaro apparently did have a disagreement with Goro-*san* the afternoon that fire broke out.

"I went to see the apothecary to find out if the rest of the story was true as well."

"Did Yuki-*san* also tell you why Kintaro yelled at Goro-*san*?" Father Mateo asked.

"She said the boy claimed Goro did not pay him," Sora said. "I wish Kintaro had told me. It might not have prevented the fire but ... who knows?"

"You did not think to confirm that the boy was paid?" The Jesuit's tone implied that Sora should have.

The guild master shook his head. "I had no reason to suspect Goro-*san* would mistreat Kintaro. He was a lazy man, but not a cheat. At least, not that I knew."

"Where did you hear this rumor about Kintaro?" Father Mateo asked. "Everyone we speak with seems to think him a helpful, diligent boy."

"It was actually Eiko-*san* who heard it," Sora admitted, "from a woman at the—"

"Where is the shinobi?" A loud, male voice demanded.

Hiro spun around.

Hiyoshi approached the bookshop at an aggressive pace. The dōshin carried the blackened swords from the fire scene, and wore a look of triumph on his face.

Father Mateo stepped in front of Hiro. "Who, precisely, do you mean?"

"Ishii." Hiyoshi came to a stop beside the priest. "He is under arrest ... for the murder of Saionji Yasuari."

"Who?" Hiro pretended not to know the name.

Hiyoshi pointed at Sora. "Your guild is harboring an assassin. Where is the spy? I demand that you turn him over to me immediately!" He raised the blackened swords. "The samurai in the fire was a member of the daimyō's personal guard, a master swordsman of the Yoshioka School named Saionji Yasuari.

"The day before his death, Yasuari-*san* warned the daimyō that a shinobi had infiltrated Edo, but he did not know the assassin's true identity. Clearly, Ishii—although I doubt that is his real name—killed Yasuari-*san* in an attempt to prevent exposure.

"We must arrest the spy at once, before he gets away."

"How did you—" the priest began.

"There is no time!" Hiyoshi slipped out of his sandals and stepped up into Sora's shop. "I must arrest him immediately, before he flees."

Hiro stepped out of his shoes and into the shop, with Father Mateo close behind.

Farther inside the building, a woman gave a startled shriek. A baby wailed. Its cries grew louder as Sora's wife emerged through the curtain that separated the shop from the living area beyond. She carried a swaddled, crying infant in her arms. "Sora-*san*—"

Hiyoshi waved his hand as he charged toward her. "Clear the way!"

She stepped aside. "Sora—"

"Later. Watch the shop." The guild master followed the dōshin through the noren.

Hiro and Father Mateo had barely reached the flapping curtain when Hiyoshi's cry of anger split the air.

Hiro jumped backward as the dōshin barreled back into the shop.

"You are under arrest!" Hiyoshi stabbed a finger at Eiko. "Your husband too! You allowed a dangerous criminal to escape!"

Eiko clutched the infant close and backed into the corner. The baby's wails grew even louder.

"Where is he!" Hiyoshi demanded.

Sora returned through the curtain. "Please, there must be a reasonable explanation—"

Hiyoshi rounded on the bookseller. "Of course there is an explanation. *He is guilty, and he fled to avoid arrest!*"

"I tried to tell you." Eiko sounded on the verge of tears. "He pushed past me—I had gone for water—when I came back, Ishii-*san* pushed me into the wall and ran off down the alley."

Hiyoshi shifted the ruined swords to his left hand. With his right, he grabbed for Sora's wrist. "You and your wife are under arrest!"

Eiko gave a cry of alarm.

The baby screamed, its small face red with rage.

"Please." Father Mateo raised his hands. "Let's talk this over reasonably."

Hiyoshi set the swords on a nearby table, pulled a slender rope from his obi, and began to tie it around Sora's wrists.

The bookseller stood motionless, head bowed in shame.

"Be reasonable." Father Mateo's voice held a warning edge.

Hiyoshi ignored him.

"I said STOP!"

The Jesuit's unexpected shout startled everyone—including the infant, who trembled in his mother's arms for the space of a breath and then resumed his furious shrieks.

"I appreciate your efforts," Sora said, "but please do not interfere on my behalf. I made an oath to the magistrate. Ishii has fled. I must accept the consequences."

"No!" Eiko took a hesitant step toward the dōshin. "Please, have mercy. This is not his fault."

"Be silent, woman," Hiyoshi snapped. "You are under arrest as well."

"She is not." Father Mateo stepped in front of Eiko. "I disagree with you arresting Sora-san, but I acknowledge that he took an oath. I will discuss my opinion of his situation with the magistrate. Eiko-san took no such oath. Her arrest, I cannot allow."

Hiyoshi finished securing the last of the knots around Sora's wrists. Still clutching the loose end of the rope, he retrieved the swords and turned to face the priest. "Magistrate Hōjō may have placed you in charge of the investigation, but I bear the authority of the Edo police. If you attempt to interfere, I will arrest you also."

CHAPTER 33

Hiro stepped into the dōshin's line of sight and laid a hand on the hilt of his wakizashi. "I humbly suggest that you stop threatening the priest."

"Your foreign master is obstructing justice," Hiyoshi declared. "By law I have the right to arrest him too."

"He carries the rank of samurai," Hiro countered. "By law, he has the right to challenge you."

"A challenge? Ha!" Hiyoshi squinted at Father Mateo. "He does not even wear a sword."

"He does not need to," Hiro said. "My blades are his to command."

"Surely we have better things to do than waste our time on ridiculous arguments," Father Mateo said. "If we move fast, we might still catch Ishii before he gets away."

Hiro knew the priest was wrong. No assassin who wanted to lose himself in Edo's warren of twisting, crowded alleys would be found if he had more than a minute's lead on his pursuers.

Hiyoshi put words to Hiro's thoughts. "We will never find him. He has vanished, like the shadows his kind are named for. All we can do now is insist that the guarantor bear his penalty." He yanked on the rope. "Come. We're going to the magistrate."

"What about Eiko-*san*?" Father Mateo raised his voice again, this time to be heard above the baby's cries.

Hiyoshi squinted at the woman. "I will leave her here for now. But if she helped the spy escape, her life will answer for it also."

Hiyoshi insisted that Sora march ahead of them through the streets. Each time they approached a crowd, the dōshin shouted, "Stand aside! Make way for my prisoner!"

Each time, the bystanders scattered like mice before a broom. Nearby shopkeepers ducked their heads and hurried about their business, sneaking sidelong looks at Sora. Even the samurai stepped aside and glared at the prisoner in disgust, as if offended to share the road with a common criminal.

Sora walked through the streets with his shoulders straight and his head held high. Except for the rope that bound his wrists like a tether on an unruly dog, he could have been out for a pleasant morning stroll.

Hiro wondered at the guild master's lack of visible emotion. Few men—aside from shinobi—had the ability to hide their thoughts so well.

He glanced at Hiyoshi, who carried the prisoner's rope in one hand and the blackened swords in the other. A foolish decision, in Hiro's mind: a man with both hands occupied could not draw his own sword, should the need arise. Clearly, the dōshin's nearsightedness ran deeper than his eyes alone.

"This is a waste of time," Father Mateo complained to Hiro in Portuguese. "We should be looking for Ishii, and for Kintaro."

Hiro replied in the Jesuit's language. "We don't have to go with them to the magistrate."

"We do if we want him to stay alive." Father Mateo nodded curtly in Sora's direction, and spoke in a tone that left no room for argument.

Not that Hiro would have argued anyway.

"Hiyoshi-*san*," the Jesuit asked as they rounded yet another curve in the road, "tell us again how you learned the identity of the victim?"

"I haven't even told you once," the dōshin retorted, "and won't, until we reach the magistrate. I solved this mystery, not you, and I intend to get the credit for it."

"I have no intention of stealing your accolades," Father Mateo said.

"Then you can wait a few more minutes to hear the tale."

A pair of broad-shouldered samurai in lacquered breastplates stood on guard beside the massive gates that marked the entrance to the magistrate's compound. As Hiro and the others neared the entrance, Father Mateo gestured toward a large man wearing brown hakama and a padded jacket, standing beside the guards. "Isn't that Daisuke?"

"It should be." Hiyoshi craned his neck to squint around Sora. "I told the commander of the daimyō's guard to send a message asking Daisuke-*sama* to meet me here."

The fire commander watched them coming with a puzzled expression on his face. As they arrived he said, "That is not the bookbinder."

"No," Hiyoshi agreed. "The shinobi heard me coming and ran away."

Daisuke sighed and shook his head. "Why am I not surprised."

"You will be, when you hear what I discovered," Hiyoshi said. "I solved the crime. All by myself. You will hear the entire tale, when I tell the magistrate."

"I can hardly wait." Daisuke's tone suggested otherwise.

"I have an important prisoner for Magistrate Hōjō," Hiyoshi announced to the armored guards. "I request a private audience with the magistrate."

The closest armored samurai shook his head. "No morning audiences today. Come back this afternoon."

"I arrested this man on Magistrate Hōjō's orders," Hiyoshi said. "He will want to see me. This concerns the recent fires in the booksellers' street. Tell him Dōshin-Investigator Hiyoshi has made a very important arrest in a very important case."

The armored guards exchanged a look. The one who had not spoken shrugged as if to say "*It's your decision.*"

The first guard sighed. "Wait here. I will ask if he will see you."

The guard disappeared through the gate. When he returned a few minutes later, he ushered them all across the yard to a flight of wooden stairs at the entrance to the magistrate's mansion.

A samurai in dark robes and white tabi waited just inside the door at the top of the stairs. He nodded to the guard, who bowed and turned away on his heel, leaving Hiro and the others to remove their shoes and follow the dark-robed samurai inside.

Without a word, the samurai led them through the outer rooms, the only sound the creaking of the wooden floors beneath their feet. Eventually, he stopped beside a sliding door, which he drew open to reveal a large reception room. Pristine tatami covered the floor. A mural of painted plum trees bloomed perpetually on the paneled walls. Two-thirds of the way across the room, a single step led up to an elevated space where the magistrate would sit while receiving guests. Although not quite as formal as the dais upon which he rendered judgments, the raised platform let the magistrate maintain a formal distance from the people he received.

The dark-robed samurai stepped across the threshold and made a gesture that encompassed the lower portion of the room. "Please wait here. Magistrate Hōjō will see you shortly."

Hiyoshi scowled. "Where is the shirazu? This man is a prisoner. There must be some mistake—"

"Magistrate Hōjō does not make mistakes." The samurai slid the door closed behind them and crossed the room to the step that separated the lower portion of the room from the magistrate's platform. In a single, practiced move, he stepped up onto the elevated area, turned to face Hiro and the others, and lowered himself to a kneeling position. He adjusted his swords, smoothed a miniscule wrinkle from his sleeve, and then rested his hands on his thighs. His face fell into patient, neutral lines.

Father Mateo walked directly to the center of the room.

Hiro suppressed a smile as the Jesuit knelt directly opposite the place where the magistrate would surely sit. He barely had time to wonder if Hiyoshi would realize what the priest had done before the dōshin started forward.

"No, no, no." Hiyoshi shook his head. "The prisoner must kneel at the center of the room, in front of the magistrate."

Father Mateo looked up, his expression unreadable. "Did you just ask a man of samurai rank to move so a merchant could sit down?" He said the word *merchant* in perfect imitation of a samurai sneer.

Hiyoshi scowled. "The prisoner—"

Father Mateo cut him off. "I heard what you said. Did you hear me?"

Instead of answering, Hiyoshi pulled Sora across the tatami to the Jesuit's right. "Kneel here. Did you hear me? On your knees!"

Sora knelt and rested his bound hands in his lap.

Hiyoshi dropped to his knees behind his prisoner, crossed his arms, and glared at the back of Father Mateo's head.

Hiro and Daisuke exchanged a look that made it clear neither man intended to kneel first.

Hiro doubted Daisuke presented any real threat—especially in such close proximity to a magistrate—but would not act on an assumption that gave anyone a tactical advantage.

At that moment, a tiny door at the far side of the room slid open.

"Magistrate Hōjō," the dark-robed samurai announced, and bowed his forehead almost to the floor.

Hiro dropped to his knees. Beside him, Daisuke did the same.

He was kneeling farther from Father Mateo than he would have liked, but Hiro recognized the time for choice had passed.

CHAPTER 34

S ora bowed his forehead to the floor as Magistrate Hōjō entered
the room and crossed to the center of the elevated platform. Hiro
and the others bowed as well, although their faces stopped short of
the floor.

The magistrate settled himself in a kneeling position directly
opposite Father Mateo. He surveyed the small assembly silently as he
arranged his robes. His gaze settled on Sora, the only one who had not
returned to a kneeling position.

After several seconds, Magistrate Hōjō asked, "What heinous
crime demands the interruption of my calligraphy practice?"

"Honorable Magistrate," Hiyoshi said. "I have solved the mystery
of the recent fires, and the samurai's murder also. You will be pleased
to learn that you did not err in ruling the first two fires accidental, or
in requesting investigation of the last. In your great wisdom—"

"Dumplings over flowers," the magistrate said. "Explain why Sora-
san kneels before me, bound like a common thief."

Hiyoshi raised the blackened swords. "Honorable Magistrate,
early this morning I took these weapons to the commander of the
daimyō's forces, and I learned the identity of their owner."

Magistrate Hōjō gave Daisuke a curious look. "The swords were
not too badly burned to identify after all?"

"Commander Imagawa did not try to identify the swords themselves," Hiyoshi said. "He did not need to. A member of the daimyō's
personal guard disappeared two nights ago, and has not returned.
Commander Imagawa feared that something terrible had happened,
because the man in question was both loyal and reliable. More importantly, that very guard had recently warned the commander that an
enemy assassin—*a shinobi*—had infiltrated Edo."

"Did Imagawa-*san* give you the name of this loyal, missing guard?" the magistrate asked.

Hiyoshi looked smug. "Saionji Yasuari. You may find it interesting to note that Yasuari-*san* was killed the very day Commander Imagawa ordered him to capture—or kill—the shinobi."

"Commander Imagawa told you this?" Magistrate Hōjō seemed surprised. "I have heard nothing about this alleged spy, or a missing guard."

"The honorable daimyō ordered all of this kept secret," Hiyoshi said. "He did not want the spy to learn that his presence had been discovered, and escape before he could be killed."

The magistrate looked doubtful, but the words rang true in Hiro's ears. Yasuari's official position among the guards suggested the Iga shinobi had come to Edo to protect the daimyō—whether or not the daimyō knew of Yasuari's true identity.

"How does this end with Sora bound before me?" Magistrate Hōjō asked.

"When I left Commander Imagawa, I went directly to this man's shop"—Hiyoshi twitched the rope that bound Sora's hands—"to arrest the bookbinder, but Ishii fled when he heard me coming. Clearly, he is the spy!"

"With respect," Father Mateo said, "none of the evidence you presented proves his guilt."

"I have not finished!" Hiyoshi reached into his obi and withdrew a slender slip of paper. "Commander Imagawa let me search Yasuari's quarters. I found this among his personal effects." He brandished the narrow slip triumphantly before offering it to the Jesuit.

Father Mateo examined the paper closely. "A receipt?"

"A claim ticket," Hiyoshi corrected, "for binding a manuscript. See? It bears Ishii's seal."

Sora pushed himself to a sitting position. His face revealed alarm.

The priest looked at the magistrate. "It does seem genuine."

"May I see it?" Magistrate Hōjō extended his hand.

The samurai at the edge of the platform stood, retrieved the slip from Father Mateo, and passed it to the magistrate before returning to his original position.

Magistrate Hōjō examined the paper carefully. "The date of delivery is the day after tomorrow." He looked up. "Why would Yasuari-*san* go to the shop ahead of schedule?"

"That's what proves Ishii is the shinobi," Hiyoshi said. "Clearly, Yasuari-*san* discovered the truth and went to confront the spy."

"Alone?" the magistrate's tone suggested doubt.

"Some men possess an overconfident view of their own abilities," Daisuke said.

Hiro resisted the urge to glance at the larger man.

"You are missing the point!" Hiyoshi declared. "I discovered who the dead man was. I discovered who killed him—"

"I respectfully disagree." Father Mateo gestured to the paper in the magistrate's hand. "That slip suggests this samurai did business with Ishii, but I understand that many samurai did so. It does not prove Ishii was a spy, or that he murdered anyone. It also fails to address the real question: who set fire to Ishii's shop?"

"Ishii did!" Hiyoshi's tone suggested this should have been obvious. "He burned his own shop to hide the body and cover his escape."

"But he did not escape," Father Mateo said. "He could have done so, easily, either on the night of the fire or the morning after. Yet he stayed to face the magistrate."

"Until we had proof that tied him to his victim," Hiyoshi said, "and then he fled at once."

The magistrate looked down at the slip of paper. "I must admit—"

He was interrupted by a sudden knock on the frame of the outer door. A moment later, the door slid open. One of the armored samurai from the gate stood in the hall.

"I humbly apologize for the interruption, Honorable Magistrate," he said. "This man insisted that I bring him here immediately."

He stepped aside, and Ishii took his place.

Hiyoshi sprang to his feet. "Seize that man before he gets away!"

Daisuke and Hiro leaped to their feet as well, but neither moved, each waiting for the other to react.

Ishii fell to his knees inside the room and pressed his forehead to the floor. "Have mercy, Honorable Magistrate. Please—give me a chance to speak before you rule."

"He murdered a samurai!" Hiyoshi declared. "He fled from justice! He deserves no mercy!"

"Enough!" Magistrate Hōjō raised his hand. "He may have fled, but he also returned of his own accord. I will hear what he has to say."

Hiyoshi pressed his lips together angrily.

The magistrate's tone softened only a fraction as he said, "Ishii, rise and approach."

The bookbinder trembled as he raised his face and then rose slowly to his feet. He made no sound as he crossed the tatami to stand beside Father Mateo, who still knelt on the floor. The Jesuit moved sideways, offering Ishii the space directly in front of the magistrate.

The bookbinder knelt and pressed his forehead to the floor again before pushing himself back up to a kneeling position. "Thank you for your mercy, Honorable Magistrate."

"You may wish to save your thanks until you hear my judgment," Magistrate Hōjō said. "Now, tell your tale."

CHAPTER 35

"I did not flee to avoid arrest," Ishii began.

"Your feet started running without your consent?" Hiyoshi asked.

Magistrate Hōjō glared at the dōshin. "You may speak when he has finished. Until then, you will be silent. And sit down. All of you—sit down."

Hiyoshi gave a startled blink and dropped to his knees.

Hiro and Daisuke knelt as well. Behind them, the door slid closed as the guard departed.

Magistrate Hōjō turned his attention to Ishii. "You may continue."

"I did not intend to flee," the bookbinder repeated, "but I panicked when I heard the dōshin say I murdered Yasuari-*san*. I knew him, but I did not kill him. Until that moment, I had no idea he was the samurai in the fire. I bound a number of manuscripts for him. He copied some of them himself. He had lovely calligraphy. I swear, I am not a spy."

Hiyoshi drew an anticipatory breath but let it out again, the words unspoken.

"I am told that, before his death, Yasuari-*san* warned the daimyō of an assassin," Magistrate Hōjō said. "Do you know anything about this matter?"

"I don't know anything about shinobi," Ishii said. "Nothing at all. I swear. I am just a simple man who wants to work in solitude."

"With respect," Sora offered, "it is not a crime for a man to prefer his own company to that of others."

"Perhaps," the magistrate replied, without shifting his gaze from the bookbinder. "However, it troubles me that you chose to run away."

"I apologize." Ishii clasped his hands. "I was terrified. I didn't stop to think. I feared, if I was arrested, I would not be allowed to prove my innocence."

The magistrate's expression hardened. "Do you hold me in such low esteem?"

"No!" Ishii's hands flew up to shield his mouth. When the magistrate did not react to the sudden shout, the bookbinder lowered his hands and his voice, and continued, "Your fairness and mercy surpass those of any magistrate I have ever heard of. But, with respect, even you require evidence."

"Fleeing arrest is compelling evidence of guilt," the magistrate observed.

"But I returned," Ishii pleaded. "I did not run away. I merely went to obtain the evidence I needed to prove I did not kill the samurai or burn my shop."

"And where is this evidence that proves your innocence?" Hiyoshi demanded.

The magistrate looked stern, but let the question stand.

Ishii looked at the floor. "Regrettably, the evidence I need has disappeared."

"Did it run away too?" Hiyoshi asked in a scathing tone.

"As a matter of fact, it did," Ishii replied. "But I can explain . . ."

"Please do." Magistrate Hōjō raised the receipt. "You may begin with this."

The dark-robed samurai retrieved the receipt from the magistrate and passed it to Ishii, who studied the paper for several seconds. "This is Yasuari-*san*'s claim slip. How did you come to possess it?" Without waiting for an answer, he continued, "This relates to a book I was binding for Yasuari-*san*—in fact, the one he came to my shop to ask about two days ago—the afternoon before the fire occurred. He stopped by the shop to ask about my progress, and confirm that I would finish the work on time. I assured him I would finish the book as promised, and he left, unharmed and very much alive.

"My apprentice, Kintaro, was with me in the shop that afternoon. He heard the conversation, and saw Yasuari-*san* arrive and leave. He can also attest that I remained in the shop for the rest of the afternoon and evening, and that Yasuari-*san* did not return.

"When I ran away from Hiyoshi-*san*, that's where I went—to get the boy, but it seems Kintaro has disappeared."

"He speaks the truth," Sora said, "at least with regard to Kintaro. He ran away from my sister's home yesterday evening. She spent half the night looking for him, to no avail. As of this morning he had not returned."

"Does the boy have a history of running off?" the magistrate asked.

"No." Sora drew the word out a fraction longer than necessary.

"Why do you hesitate?" Magistrate Hōjō gestured to Ishii. "This man's life may depend on the child's testimony. Do you know where Kintaro is?"

"No," Sora repeated, with more confidence. "With respect, I hesitated because, although I do not think the boy has run away before, I do not know for certain."

"Do you know where the child might have gone?" Magistrate Hōjō asked.

Father Mateo gave the guild master a hard look, as if wishing he would not answer.

"No," Sora said, "but I recently learned that Kintaro carried a grudge against his former master, Goro-*san*, and that the boy bought camphor from an apothecary the day before Goro-*san*'s shop caught fire. The apothecary says he made the purchase with permission, but—"

"Camphor paste is flammable." Hiyoshi's eyes went wide. "The child might have set that fire! And you said nothing!"

"There is no evidence that Kintaro set that fire, or any other," Sora said, "and I knew nothing of this until after he disappeared."

Hiro suspected that timing might not be precisely accurate, but felt no need to intervene.

Father Mateo felt otherwise. "No one I spoke with thought Kintaro set that fire, or any other. More importantly, the boy could not have killed a master swordsman of the Yoshiko school."

An awkward silence followed.

"What school?" Magistrate Hōjō asked.

"The *Yoshioka* school," Hiyoshi corrected.

"Forgive my interruption," Daisuke said, "but, despite his linguistic failure, the foreigner makes a valid point. In my experience, the simplest explanation for a fire is almost always the correct one. I suspect that goes for other crimes as well. What makes more sense: a ten year-old child setting a shop on fire and killing a samurai, or a dispute between a merchant and a nobleman that ended badly, after which the merchant panicked and set fire to his own shop to hide the crime?"

"To tell the truth, neither option strikes me as all that likely," Magistrate Hōjō said. "Why would a man destroy his home and business to hide a corpse? Men do illogical things when panicked but, even so, I find that theory hard to believe. Moreover, he claims his apprentice was with him on the day in question."

"A claim he cannot substantiate," Hiyoshi pointed out, "because the boy has conveniently disappeared."

"A claim we cannot disprove, for that same reason," Father Mateo added. "Moreover, we spoke with Ishii-*san*'s neighbors. None of them heard an argument, or anything out of the ordinary, on the afternoon in question."

"What if the argument, and the killing, did not take place inside the shop?" Daisuke gestured to Ishii. "I understand this man has a storehouse in the adjacent block."

"I do have a *kura*," the bookbinder confirmed, "and Yasuari-*san* did go there with me, on the afternoon in question, to see his manuscript, but I swear he left unharmed."

"Why hasn't anyone mentioned this before?" Hiyoshi demanded. "We must inspect that storehouse!"

"The kura holds nothing but manuscripts, and the tools I use to bind them," Ishii said. "Nothing inside has any relevance to the fire, or to Yasuari-*san*'s death."

"Then you will have no objection to a search," Daisuke said.

"Please, search for Kintaro instead," Ishii pleaded. "The kura will prove nothing, but the boy can prove my innocence."

"I have decided." Magistrate Hōjō shifted his gaze to Daisuke. "I want that storehouse searched immediately. Do it now."

Sora bowed. "Honorable Magistrate, may I ask a favor?"

Magistrate Hōjō nodded consent.

Sora raised his hands. "I did not resist arrest. I give you my word, I will not flee . . ."

"Hiyoshi-*san*, release this man—and bind Ishii." The magistrate's expression hardened. "Under the circumstances, I think it wise to ensure he does not . . . panic . . . again until we know for certain what his storehouse does or does not hold."

CHAPTER 36

Hiro and Father Mateo accompanied Daisuke, Hiyoshi, Sora, and the unhappily bound Ishii to a large plot of land adjacent to the street where Ishii's shop once stood. The lot was filled with blocky storehouses, constructed in careful rows. The newer kura were made of stone and mortar, while the older ones resembled massive earthen bricks set lengthwise on the ground. A larger firebreak surrounded the outer edges of the lot, and a well with several buckets sat in the open area at the center of the block to which the lot belonged.

Ishii led the group to one of the newer storehouses. Its sloping tiled roof lay nearly flat atop the square stone walls. The structure had no windows and only a single, narrow door set in the center of the southward-facing side.

When they reached the door, Ishii made a gesture to the simple lock that secured the entrance. "I forgot—I cannot open it. The key was in my shop when the fire broke out."

"What a convenient time to remember," Daisuke said.

"I truly did forget," Ishii insisted.

"Back away." Hiyoshi pushed the prisoner aside. "I will handle this." He examined the lock and then removed a narrow pin from his obi. He stuck the pin into the lock, wiggled it slightly, and the lock popped open.

The dōshin stepped away from the door. "It's open now."

"Why would anyone secure valuable goods with a lock that flimsy?" Father Mateo murmured in Portuguese.

"The lock is merely a formality," Hiro whispered back, in kind. "Everyone in the neighborhood probably knows who owns these storehouses, and would report a theft."

Ishii stepped between the dōshin and the door. "I must ask you, please, do not touch anything inside. Some of the items in this kura cannot be replaced, and the most valuable ones do not belong to me."

"You are in no position to make demands," Hiyoshi retorted.

"However," Daisuke offered, "we can let you handle any manuscripts we need to look behind or underneath. Will that suffice?"

"Thank you." Ishii opened the storehouse door.

The darkened space beyond was barely tall enough for a man to stand upright. Rows of shelves lined the thick stone walls, with a single, narrow passage down the center. Only the shelves closest to the entry were visible in the light that spilled through the narrow doorway, but they looked quite full and carefully organized.

"Back away," Hiyoshi ordered the bookbinder as he walked to the open door. He bent through the opening and squinted into the shadows. "Someone get a lantern. We need light."

"No!" Ishii exclaimed. When he recovered from his initial panic, he continued more calmly, "With respect, I cannot allow a flame. You may go inside, of course, and I will bring out anything you wish to see in better light, but no lanterns. No fire of any kind."

Hiyoshi peered inside again. "I can't see anything at all without a lantern."

"And not much more, even with one," Daisuke added. "Step aside. I can see just fine."

Hiyoshi did not move. "This search was my idea. I want the credit for the evidence we find."

"And you can have it," Daisuke replied, "but no one's finding anything until you step aside."

Hiyoshi cleared the door. "Make sure you bring out everything that is suspicious."

Daisuke bent to enter the storehouse, paused, and turned back to face Ishii. "Do you have anything illegal or dangerous stored inside? Or anything else that requires an explanation? Tell me now."

"Only my savings—the box of coins on the lower shelf at the very back," Ishii replied. "I earned it fairly, through hard work. The coins are mine."

"Nothing else?" Daisuke asked.

"No, nothing." Ishii shook his head. "Just tools and manuscripts."

Daisuke squeezed through the tiny door and entered the storehouse. Once inside, he had to turn sideways to navigate the narrow passage. He spent several minutes looking through the shelves adjacent to the door before moving farther into the shadowed space.

"I see nothing unusual," he called from inside. "Manuscripts, ledgers. Stacks of . . . are these boards?"

"Unfinished cover plates," Ishii said. "I put fabric over them and bind them to the manuscripts, as covers."

"I see binding thread, and pots of . . ." A grating clink, reminiscent of moving pottery, issued from inside the storehouse. "Is this glue?"

"Don't touch that. Please—" Ishii moved toward the doorway as, inside, the sounds continued.

"That one's glue, and this . . ." Daisuke sniffed, and then began coughing sharply. When he recovered, he asked, "Is this camphor paste?"

"It keeps the bugs away," Ishii replied.

"Just how large are the insects in your storehouse?" Daisuke returned to the doorway, holding a covered ceramic vessel the size of a small stew pot. He balanced the jar in his right hand as he used the left to raise the lid.

The pungent scent of camphor filled the air.

Hiyoshi squinted into the pot and promptly backed away, blinking wildly from the fumes. "The pot's half empty!"

"Half . . ." Ishii shook his head. "That cannot be."

"See for yourself." Daisuke tilted the vessel. "The amount that's missing could start an impressive fire. Several fires, in fact."

"I use camphor to keep pests away from the manuscripts," Ishii explained again. "I didn't realize how much I'd used, but . . ."

"Hold this." Daisuke replaced the lid on the pot of camphor paste and handed the vessel to Hiyoshi, who accepted it awkwardly, still clutching the rope that bound Ishii.

"I'm going back inside." The large man disappeared into the storehouse.

For a couple of minutes, Hiro heard only the careful shuffle of Daisuke's feet.

Ishii looked worried.

Hiyoshi's eyes had filled with tears from the camphor fumes. He blinked and squinted like an owl in the sun.

"Did something spill on the floor back here?" Daisuke's voice sounded muffled, and closer to the ground than usual. "The earth looks strangely dark, and feels sticky."

"I—I don't know," Ishii stammered. "Last summer, when it rained, I found a leak near that back corner, but the mason promised it was fixed."

For a minute or two, Daisuke did not reply.

A rattling came from inside the storehouse.

"What's this box?" Daisuke called. "It's near the dark spot on the floor. It looks like . . . sticks?"

"Sticks?" Ishii echoed.

"In this wooden box against the wall, at the very back. There's not enough light to see, and it's too large to carry out."

Understanding spread across Ishii's face. "Oh! I know the box you mean. That's just old tools—brushes, measuring sticks, and spatulas for spreading glue. I store the old ones in that box until I can dispose of them."

"Bookbinding tools?" Daisuke repeated.

"Yes, old tools," Ishii repeated. "Rulers, spatulas . . . maybe a paper knife or two, of the kind I use to even the edges of the manuscripts. But nothing—"

Footsteps approached the door as Daisuke returned. This time, he held a cylindrical object the length of his forearm. At first glance, it looked like a piece of lacquered bamboo cane.

"I don't think that dark spot on the floor has anything to do with leaky walls." Daisuke bent to clear the doorway and stepped out of the storehouse. When he had sufficient room to move, he gripped the cylinder in both hands and drew his hands apart, revealing the vicious-looking dagger concealed within the bamboo sheath.

Rusty stains discolored the length of the weapon's blade.

"This does not look like a paper knife to me," Daisuke said.

"That isn't mine!" Ishii exclaimed. "I don't—I swear, I've never seen that knife before!"

Daisuke considered the *tantō*. "With this much blood on the blade, I suspect that's blood on the floor inside as well. I believe we have just found our murder scene."

CHAPTER 37

Ishii grabbed hold of the rope that bound his hands and pulled the free end out of Hiyoshi's grip.

The dōshin also lost his grip on the ceramic pot. The vessel fell and shattered, spattering the ground and everyone nearby with camphor paste.

Ishii tried to run, but slipped and fell face down in the slimy mess.

Hiro dropped his knee onto Ishii's back. He clamped his hand on the bookbinder's neck and held the bald man down.

"Is that necessary?" Father Mateo asked. "He isn't struggling."

"If he is what the evidence suggests," Hiro replied, "I will take no chances."

"Please," Ishii begged. "I'm not a killer. I have never seen that tantō in my life!"

"We have the weapon, and the camphor paste he used to start the fire." Hiyoshi looked at the ruined pot. "Or at least, we can all attest the camphor paste was here." He pointed a finger at Ishii. "That man is the killer, and the one who set the fire. This mystery is solved!"

"Please, I am not a killer!" Ishii pleaded. "The camphor paste was mine, but I did not start the fire and I most certainly did not murder Yasuari-*san*. This is all a big mistake."

"Save your words for the magistrate," Hiyoshi snapped.

"Take the bookbinder to the jail," Daisuke said. "He will get no chance to escape again."

"The jail?" Hiyoshi asked. "Not to the magistrate?"

"Under the circumstances, Magistrate Hōjō will wish to arrange a public execution," Daisuke explained, "and spread the word so people can attend. This murderer will face the magistrate, and the king of hell, tomorrow."

Unless he meets with an accident tonight, Hiro thought—which, knowing Daisuke, seemed much more likely.

Ishii gave a strangled sob.

"You see?" Daisuke said. "He makes no claims of innocence now."

"I *am* innocent." Ishii raised tear-filled eyes to Sora. "Please, I beg you. Find Kintaro. Only he can save me now."

The guild master stared at the bloody knife.

"Enough." Daisuke made a dismissive gesture. "Take this man away."

Hiro released his grip on Ishii and stood up as Hiyoshi retrieved the trailing end of the rope and tied a large knot in the end to secure his grip.

"You heard the fire commander," the dōshin ordered. "On your feet."

Ishii pushed himself up onto his knees and then to his feet. He looked defeated, and said no more, as he followed Hiyoshi past the blocky storehouses toward the street.

Sora bowed to Daisuke. "I apologize. I had no idea..."

"It is not your fault," the fire commander said. "Shinobi are masters of deception. However, you must appear at the magistrate's hearing tomorrow morning. Do not forget."

"Will the magistrate punish Sora *san*?" Father Mateo asked.

"That decision lies with Magistrate Hōjō," Daisuke replied. "But, for my part, I will request no penalty."

"Thank you, Daisuke-*sama*. I am deeply grateful." Sora paused. "May I... that is, if there is nothing more..."

"You may go." Daisuke waved a dismissive hand and turned to shut the door to Ishii's storehouse.

Sora hurried off without a backward glance.

"Do we need to search the storehouse any further?" Father Mateo asked. "Perhaps there is more evidence inside."

"We need no more to prove Ishii's guilt." Daisuke relocked the door. "Between the knife and his attempt to run, no doubt remains. I would like to kill him personally, for what he did to Yasuari, but a public execution will suffice."

When Hiro and Father Mateo emerged from the warren of storehouses onto the earthen road, the Jesuit turned toward the river.

"Where are you going?" Hiro asked, although he suspected he knew the answer.

"To find Kintaro. Or, at least, to learn what happened to him."

Hiro matched his stride to the Jesuit's. "Do you have a plan?"

"First, to talk with Yuki-*san*." Father Mateo raised his hand, palm out, as if to prevent an argument. "She may not have told Ishii-*san* all she knows."

They found Yuki sitting on a wooden stool outside her door. An untouched basket of mending sat beside her feet, but her hands sat idly in her lap as she watched the children playing in the street.

She rose as Hiro and the priest approached, her face filled with hope. "Have you any word about Kintaro?"

"Unfortunately, no," Father Mateo said.

For the first time, she seemed helpless. "I searched for him everywhere, including at the teahouse and his father's grave. I even went to his uncle's shop." Yuki wrinkled her nose. "Usaburo-*san* is a loathsome man."

"Had anyone seen Kintaro?" Father Mateo asked.

"Not since yesterday," she said. "Although it seems impossible, he has disappeared completely."

Hiro had an idea. "Where do you think he would go to hide, if he felt threatened?"

"I already searched—" She drew a sudden breath. "Is Kintaro in danger?"

"I have no evidence to support that theory." *And if he is, or was, he is likely dead.* "I simply wanted to ensure that we looked everywhere."

"And yet, you are the only one who mentioned danger. Everyone else seems to believe he ran away." Yuki's face lit up. "The river! He kept talking about watching the fishermen unload their catch, and how the foreign priest came all the way across the ocean on a ship. He said he wished he could ride a boat across the ocean. At the time, I dismissed it as a child's flight of fancy but . . . I can't believe I didn't think of it before."

"Thank you," Father Mateo said. "We will look for him at the docks."

"Should he return," Hiro added as they turned to leave, "send word to Sora-*san* at once, and do not let the boy out of your sight."

CHAPTER 38

Hiro and Father Mateo searched the docks and along the shore until the sun hung low on the horizon, but found no trace of the missing boy.

They returned to the Kaeru Ryokan as the sun set, the evening clouds ablaze with sunset's final fire.

"I just don't understand." The Jesuit peered down yet another alley as they passed. "Where did he go?"

"At this point, I think we need to accept the possibility that—"

"No!" Father Mateo's tone grew soft. "Please, do not say it yet."

Hiro respected the priest's request and finished silently—*he isn't coming back.*

Kaeru met them at the entrance to the inn. Her welcoming smile faded on her lips. "Has something happened?"

"The child we were searching for has not been found," Father Mateo said.

"Did you speak with Bin-*san*?" Kaeru asked.

"She does not think Kintaro set the fires." A defensive note crept into the Jesuit's voice.

"Then why would he run away?" Kaeru seemed confused. "People do not simply disappear without a cause. Not even children."

Hiro took pity on the priest and changed the subject. "Have you heard from Natsu-*san*?"

"Regrettably, no." Kaeru's forehead wrinkled with concern. "Perhaps you should let me deliver the message from Hanzō-*sama* on your behalf when she returns. I know how important the matter is, and I give you my word, I will tell her without delay. I think perhaps my first guess was correct, and that she's stuck behind the snow in the mountain passes. That is what I choose to believe, at least. But if that's true, it could be weeks before the thaw allows her to return, and it seems unreasonable to make you wait here until spring."

"We will consider it," Hiro said, as much to end the conversation as from any real intent to leave.

Kaeru bowed acknowledgment as Hiro followed a tired-looking Father Mateo into the ryokan and up the stairs.

The Jesuit bent his head over his Bible in silent prayer until Ana and Kaeru brought the dinner trays. Even then, he seemed half-absent, picking at his food and saying nothing.

Hiro found himself unable to enjoy the meal, which seemed a shame, given the obvious care with which it was prepared. Eventually, he sighed and said, "Please tell me what you're thinking."

Father Mateo startled as if lost in thought. "It will come as no surprise. I just keep picturing Kintaro, somewhere out there in the darkness, cold and scared . . . or worse . . ."

"We've searched for hours, last night and again today," Hiro replied. "If he's alive, he does not want to be found."

"But *why?*" the priest insisted. "Why did he run away? It makes no sense. The facts—the evidence—do not add up. We're missing something."

As much as he would have liked to argue, Hiro found he could not disagree.

"Would you do something for me?" Father Mateo asked.

Hiro raised his eyebrows expectantly and waited.

"Go look for Kintaro one last time, while I stay here and ask God to help you find him." Father Mateo hurried on as if concerned that Hiro might refuse. "Kintaro trusted you at the teahouse. He might trust you now."

"If he trusted me, he would have shown himself last night, or earlier today."

"You weren't alone," the priest replied. "Last night, you searched with Yuki-*san*. Today you searched with me. He might have been too scared to show himself."

"I hardly think—"

"Please, Hiro. One last time."

Hiro shrugged. "I will try, but I don't believe it's going to work."

At last, Father Mateo smiled. "If you will try, I trust in God to do the rest."

After the meal, Hiro put on his traveling cloak and shoes and left the ryokan.

The sun had set, and the temperature had plunged. The previous nights had not been anywhere near this cold. For Kintaro's sake, Hiro hoped the boy was not outside.

Once again, he started toward the river. He had searched it thoroughly that afternoon, with the Jesuit, but could not think of any better place to start.

As he walked, he reviewed the evidence against Ishii. The pieces fit almost too perfectly. He disliked having only a secondhand identification of the swords, along with Daisuke's word and the netsuke, to confirm Yasuari's identity.

In particular, he disliked being forced to rely on Daisuke.

He also felt a measure of chagrin at being fooled by Ishii. Hiro considered himself quite skilled at reading people, and it bothered him that he had failed to see through a spy's disguise.

When he reached the river, he turned south on the path that paralleled the bank. A little way ahead, a bridge cut a deep black arc through the darkness. Lanterns in the shops, and set at intervals along the path, cast shimmering circles on the water rushing swiftly past below. He heard it lapping at the earth and stone of the banks as it hurried past on its way to join the sea.

A peal of raucous laughter drifted out the window of a sake shop. Inside, a group of men in striped kimono knelt around a wooden table. One poured sake while another told a tale. They laughed again, reminding Hiro of the many pleasant evenings he had spent with Kazu at Ginjiro's brewery in Kyoto. He wondered when—and if—he would enjoy the careless luxury of such an evening once again.

If he ever did, he hoped he would remember to appreciate it for the gift it was.

Past the teahouses and the bridge, the path grew dark as he drew close to the fishermen's district. A row of short piers lined the riverbank. A fleet of flat-bottomed fishing boats bobbed and creaked in the current, tied up safely for the night.

On the landward side of the path, a row of houses, many little more than shacks, clustered together like barnacles on a piling. No light shone in the any of the windows. Sleep came early for the men and women who rose before dawn to ply the sea.

Hiro slowed his pace. He listened carefully for any sound that did not belong to the river or the night.

A second bridge cast its arch across the river just beyond the last of the fishing piers. As he walked toward it, Hiro's hopes of finding Kintaro faded. If Ishii was an assassin, the child's body was probably feeding the fish that would feed the people of Edo in the morning.

Hiro pushed the unpleasant thought aside.

The riverbank grew steep as he approached the bridge. The darkened path ran close to the edge, and Hiro placed his feet with care. A misstep or a trip could easily lead to a dangerous and unwanted swim.

Something rustled among the pilings on the bank beneath the bridge.

Hiro froze and listened. The shadowed area at the near end of the bridge was large enough to conceal a man, if he crawled on his hands and knees, but only a drunkard or a fool would risk a fall into the freezing water.

A shadow moved beneath the bridge and then went still.

Hiro leaned down and peered into the darkness, unwilling to move closer until he knew what made the sound.

Something moved beneath the bridge—and slipped over the side of the riverbank with an all too human—and familiar—yelp.

"Kintaro!" Hiro raced toward the river as the shadow struck the water with a splash.

By the time he reached the edge, the child had disappeared.

A moment later, a small dark head appeared above the rushing water, moving downstream fast. It bobbed for a moment, sank, and reappeared, accompanied by a pair of flailing arms.

"He—" Kintaro's head disappeared again.

Hiro pulled his swords from his obi, dropped them on the riverbank, and dove headfirst into the rushing river.

The shock of the icy water drove the breath from Hiro's lungs. He broke the surface, gasped, and exhaled convulsively.

The river was much deeper than he expected, too. Even close to the bank, his feet did not touch bottom.

Kintaro breached the surface once again, but the current carried him swiftly out of reach.

Hiro swam toward the boy as fast as possible. Around him, the river felt like liquid ice. He passed beneath the bridge and emerged on the other side just as Kintaro slipped beneath the surface yet again.

This time, the boy did not seem conscious.

Hiro lunged, and felt his fingers graze the hem of the child's robe as Kintaro sank toward the bottom like a stone.

CHAPTER 39

Hiro drew a breath and dove beneath the surface.

Darkness surrounded him, black as ink.

He pulled himself downward, one hand stretched in front of him, his fingers questing for the boy. His fingers brushed something that felt like cloth. He grabbed it and squeezed his fingers tight, hoping he had a solid enough grip to drag his burden to the surface—and that when he got there, he would find he had the child and not a fistful of river reeds.

As Hiro kicked for the surface, he felt the current sweeping him downstream. His legs felt impossibly heavy, like blocks of stone. His lungs convulsed with the instinct to draw a breath.

After what seemed far longer than the seconds that actually passed, Hiro reached the surface. He drew a gasping breath and dragged his burden upward. His knees went weak with relief when he saw Kintaro's small, dark head appear.

The emotion faded as he saw the water drain from the child's open mouth.

He could not see Kintaro breathing.

Hiro hooked his left arm around the child's upper body and used his right to swim to the riverbank. It loomed high overhead . . . too high to escape without a climb, and he could not climb while carrying the child.

He grasped the bank and looked back toward the bridge. On land, he could have thrown a rock and hit it. In the water, and against the current, it might as well have been a thousand miles away. He turned and looked downriver. The moonless night made it hard to tell where the water ended and the sky began, but he thought he saw a break in the embankment just a little way downstream.

He looked up at the riverbank again. Large stones protruded from the earth. Without Kintaro, he could make the climb.

Years of shinobi training told him to release the boy and save himself.

But Hiro couldn't do it. Not unless . . .

He moved his hand up to Kintaro's chest, and felt the whisper of a heartbeat.

Still a chance.

He kept Kintaro's face above the water as he made his way along the riverbank. The feeling faded from his fingers, which grew stiff as the nerves inside them numbed. The icy water lapped at his chin and splashed him in the face. He stared at the darkness, sorry he did not possess the faith to hope for one of the miracles Father Mateo preached as facts.

He could not even blame the deities for ignoring him.

After all, they were merely returning the favor.

His outstretched hand fell back into the water. In his numbed state, he must have lost his grip on the riverbank. Hiro reached for it, but once again, his hand met only air.

His thoughts were moving slowly too, so slowly that the current almost carried him completely past the opening in the riverbank before he recognized it as a long, shallow ramp the fishermen used for launching boats. He came to his senses just in time to grasp the stones on the downstream side of the long, shallow ramp that led from the river to the ground above.

Working one-handed, Hiro pulled himself, and then Kintaro, onto the ramp, where he discovered with surprise that the water barely reached above his knees. The current eased its grip almost at once, and Hiro hoisted Kintaro's limp, still form onto his shoulder as he struggled up the ramp to shore.

A long, flat-bottomed fishing boat sat on the bank at the top of the ramp. Although the hull sat well above the water line, the bow was tethered to a large stone post embedded in the ground.

Only as Hiro lowered Kintaro to the ground beside the post did he hear the shouting voices and the sound of feet approaching at a run.

"What's going on?" A male voice asked.

"He jumped in the river!" A second voice answered. "Bring a light!"

Hiro laid his fingers on Kintaro's neck.

He felt no pulse.

A circle of golden light illuminated the child's pale face.

"He has a child!" the first man exclaimed.

"The boy is dead," the other whispered.

Hiro closed his eyes and adjusted his fingers on Kintaro's neck. This time, he felt a tiny flutter, like the wingbeats of a dying moth.

He rolled Kintaro's body onto its side and pounded hard on the child's thin back. He lowered his mouth to Kintaro's ear and yelled, "Wake up! Open your eyes!"

"It is too late," the first man said. "The Ōgawa is too cold—"

"Wake UP!" Hiro pounded Kintaro's back again.

A moment later, the child convulsed and vomited a stream of water onto the riverbank.

Kintaro spluttered, coughed, and retched again. His eyes fluttered open. He continued to cough and heave, spitting water on the ground with each exhale.

The man with the lantern gasped in disbelief. "Did you see that?"

"He brought the child back to life!" the second man declared. "Jizō heard his prayers!"

Hiro finally turned and looked up at the men.

They wore the slime and blood-encrusted smocks of fishmongers. The taller man held a glowing lantern. Unexpectedly, his companion held a folded quilt . . . and Hiro's swords.

"You need to get inside and dry," the man with the lantern said. "You'll freeze to death quickly, out here in the cold."

As if on cue, Kintaro began to shake.

"I have a room at an inn nearby," Hiro replied, "I will take him there."

"At least take this." The man extended the folded quilt. "To keep the child warm until you get there. You don't have to bring it back."

Hiro accepted the quilt with a nod of thanks and wrapped it around Kintaro. The boy continued to shiver, cough, and sniffle.

Hiro rose to his own somewhat unsteady feet. He accepted his swords and thrust them through his obi before bending down to lift Kintaro.

Even dripping wet and covered in a quilt, the boy was unexpectedly light.

Small for his age, indeed.

"Would you like the lantern?" the tall man asked when they reached the path. "Or a physician? We can send for—"

"Thank you," Hiro said, "but I can manage."

The fishermen bowed. "You are a brave man, sir. Not many samurai would jump into the Ōgawa at night, even to save their sons."

"This boy is not my son."

As the fishermen's mouths dropped open, Hiro turned and walked away.

CHAPTER 40

Between the darkness and the cold, it felt so late that Hiro was surprised to see a dark blue noren hanging in the entrance to the bathhouse two doors down from the Kaeru Ryokan. He vaguely remembered Kaeru mentioning the bath was open late—but also realized he had lost all track of time since jumping in the river.

His kimono clung to his body, its clammy weight making him feel even colder. In his arms, Kintaro shivered like a fledgling in the snow.

Hiro ducked through the noren and opened the sliding door beyond.

A wave of warm, humid air enveloped him like a mother's hug as he stepped into the bathhouse. Just inside the door, the middle-aged proprietor stood behind a wooden counter. He looked up.

"We close in half—" The rest of the sentence died on his lips at the sight of the quilt-wrapped boy and Hiro's dripping clothes. "What happened to you? With respect . . . you look like you fell in the Ōgawa."

"As it happens . . ." Hiro trailed off as the proprietor's eyes grew large.

"Do not worry about the time, or the bathing fee." The man reached underneath the counter and withdrew a pair of narrow towels. "Please, go right inside."

Hiro slipped off his sandals, accepted the towels, and carried Kintaro through the doors into the changing room.

"Can you stand?" he asked.

When Kintaro nodded, Hiro set him down.

Without a word, the shinobi moved away from the boy, stripped off his sodden clothes, and hung them on a wooden peg. As he removed his kimono, he realized the shuriken he always kept in a hidden pocket of the sleeve had disappeared—most likely lost in the freezing water of the river.

Better my shuriken than my life.

Hiro crossed the room and took a seat on one of the low wooden stools that lined the wall. He plunged his freezing fingers into the bucket of creamy soap and lathered his skin as best he could. He rinsed the soap away with a dipper of water that, though unheated, felt far warmer than the river's icy depths.

In his eagerness to finish his ablutions and get into the steaming bath, he almost forgot Kintaro. As he started toward the bathing room, he glanced quickly down the row of stools, noting with approval that the boy was managing his own ablutions with no trouble.

Hiro passed through the doorway into the room beyond, which held an enormous cedar tub. Although it would have held two dozen men, only a single, elderly patron sat in the heated water, his folded towel perched atop his balding head as he dozed in the steaming bath.

Hiro stepped into the tub, exhaling slowly as the fiery heat of the water met his freezing skin. He lowered himself to a seated position, leaving only his head and neck above the surface. As he closed his eyes, he felt the heat of the bath seeping into his skin and leaching through his muscles, thawing him from the outside in.

Moments later, a disturbance in the water announced Kintaro's arrival at the tub. When the water calmed, Hiro opened one eye just long enough to see the boy had knelt a respectful distance from both Hiro and the other man.

Hiro closed his eye again and exhaled slowly, letting the water do its work.

After several minutes, the water swirled as the elderly patron rose to leave. Hiro exchanged a silent nod with the older man, who disappeared through the door to the outer room.

While he would have liked to stay in the water longer, Hiro knew the heat was harder for a child to bear, and Kintaro had soaked long enough to chase off any chance of a fatal chill.

"The bathhouse will be closing soon. It's time to go." Hiro stood up and left the tub.

When Hiro returned to the outer room, he found the bathhouse owner waiting, holding a pile of carefully folded clothes.

"Forgive my presumption," the proprietor said, "but I asked my wife to wash and dry your clothes. These coats and hakama are not as fine as your kimono, or even the child's tunic, but they will keep you warm enough tonight, and we will return your clothes tomorrow, if you tell us where you live, or where you're staying."

Hiro accepted the pile of clothes with a grateful nod. "Kaeru Ryokan."

"A fine establishment. My wife will bring your clothes to you tomorrow." The bathhouse owner bowed and left the room.

Hiro handed the smaller tunic and hakama to Kintaro, who put them on while Hiro dressed. As they started toward the door, the boy asked, "Does this mean I get to stay with you?"

They were the first words he had spoken since the river.

Hiro smiled. "For tonight, at least."

The heat from the bath warmed Hiro's limbs, making the cold night air feel almost pleasant as he and Kintaro walked to the ryokan.

"Tomorrow you will take me to the magistrate?" Kintaro asked.

"Tomorrow, I will take you back to Sora-*san*—"

Before Hiro could add *and Yuki*, Kintaro said, "He doesn't want me. He thinks I set the fires too."

Hiro started up the stairs at the front of the ryokan. "We can address that issue in the morning."

He half expected the boy to argue, but Kintaro simply followed him into the inn and up the creaking stairs.

Father Mateo gasped and dropped his Bible as Hiro and Kintaro entered the room. He crossed himself and asked, "Where did you find him?" Slowly, the priest's expression shifted. "Why are you wearing someone else's clothes?"

"I fell in the river," Kintaro said. "Matsui-*san* jumped in to save me."

"You jumped into the river?" Father Mateo asked.

"Would you rather I had let him drown?" Hiro replied,

"Yes!" Tears sprang to Kintaro's eyes. "I wish you let me drown!"

Father Mateo stared at the boy, aghast.

"Everybody thinks I set the fires," Kintaro wailed. "Even you—I heard you say it to Yuki-*san*. That's why I ran away. Everybody says I set the fires, but I didn't! But nobody cares. The magistrate will burn me anyway.

"I miss my Father!"

The boy collapsed on Hiro's futon, buried his face in his hands, and sobbed.

Father Mateo began to speak, but Hiro silenced the Jesuit with a look.

Kintaro's sobs had barely slowed to heaving breaths when the stairs began their telltale creaking. Hiro hoped it was Ana, but seconds later Kaeru's voice came through the door.

"I apologize for disturbing you so late . . ."

Kintaro sat upright. He gave one last, sobbing sniff and then fell silent.

"Come in, Kaeru-*san*," Father Mateo said.

When she slid the door open, the priest continued, "We apologize for disturbing you and your other guests."

"I have no other guests tonight," Kaeru said, "and it is no bother. I simply did not expect to hear a child crying. I am relieved to see Kintaro has been found."

"We will take him home tomorrow morning," Father Mateo said.

Kintaro turned to the priest, his face a mixture of worry and confusion.

"It appears you need an extra futon," Kaeru said. "I have extras in the room next door."

As Hiro followed her into the hall, Kintaro jumped to his feet. "I want to help."

The innkeeper slid the adjacent shoji open with a silent rumble.

The room beyond looked much the same as Hiro and Father Mateo's, except that it had no decoration in the tokonoma and four waist-high piles of quilts and futons lined up neatly against the wall.

"I can do it." Kintaro squeezed past Hiro and Kaeru and lifted a futon from the closest stack. "See? I can carry it myself."

Hiro followed the boy back to the room where Father Mateo waited.

Kintaro set his futon down with a gentle thump and unfolded it in the space between Hiro and Father Mateo's quilts. Kaeru handed Hiro a winter quilt before closing the door to the adjacent room.

"If you need anything more," she said, "please let me know."

"Thank you," Father Mateo called.

Kaeru bowed and retreated toward the stairs.

CHAPTER 41

As the stairs announced Kaeru's descent, Kintaro knelt on his futon, eyes still red from his recent tears.

"Kintaro," Father Mateo said as Hiro closed the guest room door. "We do not think you set the fires."

"But I know you do," the boy said earnestly. "You asked me all those questions. Then, when Yuki-*san* asked you if I set the fires, you said maybe. You said you were looking for me. I heard you say it. I was right around the corner. I was coming back from the temple and I heard you talking. I was afraid you wanted to arrest me, so I hid and listened. When I heard you say it was my fault, I ran away."

"We never said the fires were your fault," Father Mateo said. "Yuki-*san* asked us to protect you, and we agreed."

"She did?" Kintaro looked down at the futon. "I ran away before I heard that part." He looked up. "Why did you investigate me then?"

"We have to investigate every clue, not only to prove who is guilty, but also to discover who is innocent," Father Mateo said.

"It doesn't matter. Everyone thinks I'm guilty." Kintaro sniffled. "I heard Eiko-*san* say I was dangerous. She said I burned up Goro-*san*'s shop with camphor paste. But that's not true!"

"And yet, you did buy camphor paste from the apothecary," Hiro said.

"Goro-*san* told me to, and made me promise never to say why. Now he's dead, and if I break my promise, he will haunt me."

"Why would camphor paste be secret?" Father Mateo asked.

"I can't tell you," Kintaro said. "I promised."

"Did Goro use the paste to set a fire?" Hiro doubted it, but asked the question anyway.

Kintaro shook his head. "It wasn't even in his shop."

Father Mateo looked confused, but Hiro had a flash of insight. "Did Goro want you to buy the paste for someone else?"

Kintaro's mouth fell open in surprise. "How did you know?"

"How *did* you know?" Father Mateo asked.

"Goro told his friend next door—the artisan Susumu—that he should try camphor paste to help his hands. Susumu's wife refused to let him buy it, and complained about the smell." Hiro paused. "There is no way she could have smelled the camphor paste inside Goro's shop—the scent is strong, but not that strong. However, if Goro brought a pot of camphor paste along with him that night, when he visited Susumu's shop—a gift for an old friend in need—Susumu's wife might easily have smelled the paste when her husband opened it. I bet, if we confronted him outside her hearing, he would admit that Goro gave him a pot of camphor paste, and that he hides it from his wife."

"It was a gift. That's what he made me promise not to tell." Kintaro smiled, but it faded quickly. "Are you going to turn me over to the magistrate, because I lied?"

"No," Hiro said, "but Father Mateo and I do need to see the magistrate in the morning, and right now we all could use some sleep."

Father Mateo banked the fire in the brazier as Kintaro crawled beneath his quilt and laid his head down with a sigh.

Hiro set his swords on the floor beside his futon.

Kintaro's head popped up. "Matsui-*san*?"

"Yes?" Hiro paused, halfway beneath his quilt.

"Will Daisuke-*san* go to see the magistrate tomorrow morning too?"

"I believe so, why?"

"Can I go with you?" Kintaro asked. "I want to tell him that I'm sorry about his basket."

"About his basket?"

"The one he had to drop so he could save me," Kintaro said. "I feel bad, because it was my fault that it got burned."

"He does not care about the basket," Hiro said, "I heard him say so. Go to sleep."

On the far side of the room, Father Mateo's quilt and futon rustled softly as the priest lay down. The room grew still, the silence interrupted only by the gentle sound of breathing.

Hiro felt a wave of exhaustion, followed by the pull of impeding sleep. As he drifted off, he could not shake the thought that he had overlooked a vital clue, some piece of the puzzle that might change the outcome.

He sat up to clear his head, refusing to surrender to oblivion until he knew the answer. Minutes passed. The flames in the brazier slowly died. The room grew dim, then dark.

Still Hiro knelt, deep in thought, and reviewed the evidence piece by piece.

Suddenly, it all fell into place.

He reviewed the facts twice more. Each time, he reached the same conclusion.

He knew who was responsible for the crimes. More importantly, he knew *why*.

"Mateo," he whispered.

"Hiro?" The Jesuit's voice was hoarse from sleep. "What time is it?"

"Shh," Hiro whispered, "Do not wake the boy."

Father Mateo's futon rustled as the priest sat up. "What's going on?"

"I know who murdered Yasuari—and who set the fires."

CHAPTER 42

Hiro shifted to Portuguese. "Ishii is not guilty, despite the evidence Daisuke 'discovered' in the storehouse."

"Your tone suggests . . ." Father Mateo paused. "But that cannot be. We already determined Daisuke could not have set the fires. He sounded the alarm and ran to the scene with the fire brigade."

"Where he left Ryuu in charge and disappeared," Hiro replied.

"He did not disappear. He went around the back of the building to see how far the fire had spread. That's when he heard Kintaro scream."

"We were at that fire," Hiro said. "Did you hear Kintaro scream?"

"No," the priest admitted, "there was too much noise—but Daisuke was behind the building. Perhaps it was quieter there."

"Daisuke *claimed* he heard the boy from behind the building," Hiro said, "and yet Kintaro told us he was at the front of the shop— near the shutters— and that his lungs were burning from the smoke, which made it difficult to scream. If we could not hear him, there's no way his voice carried all the way to the alley behind the building."

"Then how . . ."

"Daisuke did not hear Kintaro. He saw the boy when he carried Yasuari's body into the shop, to dispose of it in the flames."

"Surely someone would have seen him carrying . . ." The priest fell silent as the realization struck him. "The body was in the basket."

"Exactly." Hiro gestured to the sleeping boy. "If Daisuke had truly left the basket outside the shop, as he claimed, Kintaro would not have seen it, and would not have known that it was lost. But Kintaro said Daisuke had to *drop* the basket, which means he carried it inside the burning shop—which he would not have done if he entered the fire to save a screaming child. The only reason he would carry a basket that size into the fire is to ensure its contents perished in the flames."

"If that's the case, why would Daisuke save the boy at all?"

"He had no choice," Hiro answered. "He could hardly risk Kintaro following him back out and claiming the commander of the fire brigade left him behind."

"He could have killed the boy . . . although, given the state of the fire, perhaps he did not have the time." Father Mateo thought for a moment. "Would a trained assassin truly risk concealing a body in a basket that belonged to the fire brigade? Anyone could have opened the lid and found it before the fire."

"He must have hidden the body elsewhere, and retrieved it after he ran to the scene with the fire brigade. He left Ryuu in charge, and ran away to retrieve the body under the guise of inspecting the perimeter of the fire.

"I suspect he has a storehouse near Ishii's, and that he ambushed Yasuari after the meeting with the bookbinder. It would have been easy enough to do in the narrow passages between the kura, and also simple to retrieve a body from the next block over without his absence being noticed at the fire. We need to find that warehouse in the morning, before we see the magistrate."

"If we can." Father Mateo sounded doubtful. "Daisuke will have used a better lock than Ishii did."

"I can handle the locks." Hiro smiled grimly. "You and Kintaro must come with me. It is not safe for you to stay alone."

"You could go tonight," the priest suggested. "We would be safe—"

"You would not, because Daisuke did not work alone. He had an accomplice, who set the fires, and if my theory is correct . . ." Hiro shook his head. "I will not leave you undefended."

"Who set the fires?" Father Mateo asked.

"I cannot answer that question without making an assumption," Hiro said, "and I would like to think it through a little more. You should get some sleep. We will leave before dawn, to find the evidence we need to save Ishii."

"You plan to expose Daisuke to the magistrate?" Father Mateo's eyes widened in surprise.

"I do not need to expose his true identity to reveal him as the killer," Hiro said, "and while I would prefer to kill him personally, that solution would not save Ishii."

The Jesuit lay back on his futon. "Thank you for that."

Hiro nodded. "Go to sleep."

Father Mateo closed his eyes, but opened them again almost immediately. "The night of the fire, Ryuu-*san* mention a second basket—one Daisuke lost almost two months ago."

"On the night of the fire at Kenji's shop," Hiro confirmed. "I suspect it held the remains of Natsu."

"Natsu is dead?" Surprise made Father Mateo's voice too loud. He covered his mouth with his hand and looked at Kintaro.

The boy shifted in his sleep, but did not wake.

Father Mateo lowered his hand and whispered, "How do you know?"

"I don't, for certain," Hiro admitted, "but her absence, combined with the fact that no one knows the identity of the woman Kenji met at night, and the fact that Daisuke has killed at least one other member of the Iga ryu . . ."

"We need to warn Kaeru." Father Mateo sat up.

"Unless I miss my guess, she already knows," Hiro replied. "You don't use a person's room for futon storage if you think they're going to return."

"But . . . that would make Kaeru the accomplice." Father Mateo sounded incredulous. "Surely you don't think she set the fires?"

"It had not occurred to me until I saw the state of Natsu's room," Hiro admitted, "but now . . . Kaeru had no guests the night of the fire at Ishii's shop, and was not here when Ana first arrived."

"She was out for a walk," Father Mateo said.

"In the dark, on a winter night?" As the words left his lips, Hiro heard a faint but familiar sound.

Father Mateo opened his mouth to speak, but Hiro raised a warning hand.

In the silence that followed, Hiro heard the sound again—the faintest squeak of a board on the stairs. He inhaled deeply. Underneath the familiar scent of wood smoke, he detected the pungency of camphor.

"Did you use your gift from Bin tonight?" he whispered.

"No, why?" The tension in Father Mateo's voice made the whispered response sound choked.

Hiro reached for his swords. He thrust the katana through his obi, but drew the shorter wakizashi silently from its sheath and set the scabbard back down on the floor.

"Don't make a sound," Hiro whispered to the priest as he rose to his feet and crept toward the door.

A faint glow of light seeped through the crack where the shoji met the wall.

There was someone in the hall.

Hiro's pulse increased. He gripped the wakizashi in his right hand. With the left, he slid the shoji open just enough to peek outside.

CHAPTER 43

D aisuke crouched in the hall outside the door to Natsu's room. A shielded lantern sat on the floor beside him. Slowly, the large shinobi dipped a brush into a pot half-filled with camphor paste and painted a thick line along the bottom of the wall.

He wore a heavily padded, hooded coat the size and shape of the protective jackets worn by the fire brigade, but the outer covering was dark instead of the customary white. Based on the lumpy, uneven seams along the shoulders, he was wearing the garment inside-out.

An easily reversible disguise.

Hiro slid the door open and stepped into the hall.

Daisuke sprang up and backward, dropping the pot and brush. He landed silently, out of reach, now with a dagger in his hand. "You don't look nearly surprised enough to see me."

"Hiro?" Father Mateo's voice held an edge of alarm.

"Stay in the room," Hiro replied, keeping his gaze on Daisuke. "No matter what you hear, do not come out the door."

"Why delay the inevitable?" Daisuke asked. "You know I came to kill the boy, and the priest as well. But you don't have to die tonight, if you make the right decisions."

"Like overlooking the fact that you're the one murdering members of the Iga ryu?" Hiro asked.

"You figured it out." Daisuke gave a grudging nod. "I admit, I didn't think you would."

"What did Oda promise you?" Hiro asked.

"The same thing you'll receive, if you join his cause. Money and power, once he claims the shogunate." Daisuke smiled. "The benefits that always come to those who serve the winning side."

"Promises and eggs are easily broken. Only a fool puts confidence in either."

"You think your cousin Hanzō is any more trustworthy?" Daisuke laughed harshly. "He can't stand you any more than I can. Sooner or later, he will have you killed."

Hiro noted a haze in the air. "Did you forget to bring a basket? Or did Kaeru tell you not to bother?"

"Once the priest and the boy are dead, there's no one left to kill." Daisuke gestured to the pot of camphor on the floor. "She going to burn the inn tonight, and then we're leaving Edo. That's why she had me spread the last of the camphor paste up here—to ensure the fire moves fast once it gets started."

"She sent you up here to ensure you would not escape." Hiro nodded toward the stairs, where a flickering orange glow had just appeared. "She betrayed you—turn around and see for yourself."

Daisuke barked a laugh. "Do you take me for a fool? If I turn, you'll stab me in the back."

"True," Hiro said, "but it's also true she already set the fire."

Daisuke sniffed the air. "She was supposed to wait until I finished."

Inside the guest room, Father Mateo said, "Wake up, Kintaro. We need to leave."

Daisuke's gaze flicked to doorway.

In that instant, Hiro leaped.

He landed directly in front of Daisuke and used the momentum from his leap to drive the tip of his wakizashi through the other shinobi's padded jacket. He felt the tip of the blade pierce through clothing, and then through flesh.

With his free hand, Hiro grabbed the front of Daisuke's jacket and pulled it forward, using the traitor's weight to force his short sword deep. His aim was true. He felt the sword slip between Daisuke's ribs and into his heart.

Daisuke's blade clattered harmlessly to the floor. His lips moved in an attempt to speak, but his mouth produced only a thick, wet sound. He coughed, and bloody droplets sprayed over Hiro's face and neck.

The lantern and the flickering orange glow by the stairs gave Hiro just enough light to see Daisuke's eyes go dark and cold as the large man's spirit fled.

An unexpected flare of rage made Hiro stab the sword into the dead man's chest twice more before releasing his grip on the jacket. Daisuke's lifeless form slumped to the floor. Hiro forced himself to resist the urge to spit on the traitor's corpse.

Instead, he returned to the guest room door. "We need to get out of here right now."

Father Mateo returned to the doorway, with Kintaro at his side. "What about Ana? We need to get her too."

Hiro looked back toward the staircase. The flames had reached the upper floor and reached into the hall like grasping hands.

"Stay here," Hiro told the priest, "I'll check the stairs."

A wave of heat struck his face as he stepped over Daisuke's corpse.

Even before he reached the stairs, he knew that it was far too late to use them. Fire engulfed the narrow opening. Huge flames filled the open space and climbed the walls, obscuring Hiro's view of the floor below.

Hiro held his sleeve across his mouth and retreated to the priest, stepping over Daisuke's body on the way. "We can't take the stairs. There's too much fire."

Father Mateo cupped his hands around his mouth. "ANA!" He yelled. "Wake up! Get ou—" The rest of his warning disappeared into a wracking cough.

"There's nothing we can do for her," Hiro said. "We can only hope she got out on her own."

"We're trapped." Kintaro sobbed.

"Not yet." Hiro gestured to the slatted window in the wall beside him. "We'll go that way."

"The slats don't open." Father Mateo coughed again.

Kintaro started coughing too.

"Get back in the room," Hiro said. "Put quilts on your heads to block the smoke while I get the window open."

Father Mateo pulled Kintaro back into the room.

I hope this works. Hiro turned his right side to the window, leaned away, and aimed a kick at the wooden slats.

The boards made a cracking sound, but held.

Hiro kicked the slats again. The lattice shook, but did not break.

At the far end of the hall, enormous flames stretched from the staircase like the arms of a giant squid. The fire groaned and crackled. Beams creaked underneath the floor, which now felt warm to Hiro's feet.

I'm out of time.

CHAPTER 44

Hiro ripped the oiled paper off the slats and looked outside. A crowd was gathering in the narrow street.

In the distance, a bell began to toll.

"Do something!" A familiar, female voice demanded.

"Ana?" Hiro pressed his face to the slats and tried to see. Between the smoke and his watering eyes, he could not be sure.

"Hiro!" Ana yelled from the street below. "Are you in there? Are you safe?"

Am I safe?

He inhaled a breath of slightly cleaner air from between the slats, stepped back, and exhaled with a yell as he kicked the boards with all the force that he possessed. He kicked again, and then again.

On the final strike, the lower end of a single slat broke free.

Hiro stopped to push it away from its neighbors, giving him more space for leverage. He drew another breath from the gap, pulled back inside, and kicked the slat beside the broken space.

The slat broke free.

A rush of air swirled into the hall as he pushed the slat aside.

Shouts rose from the crowd below. "Up there! At the window! Someone is alive!"

More voices answered.

"Get a ladder!"

"Get the fire brigade!"

Hiro stepped back from the window and kicked the next slat in the row. Now that he had the space to direct his strike against a single board, instead of the window as a whole, the slats broke much more easily.

He kicked out six more slats, until the space was large enough to get his head and shoulders through.

Thundering feet and excited shouts in the street announced the arrival of the fire brigade. Hiro stuck his head through the window and saw Ryuu giving orders to a group of men.

Ana grabbed the enormous firefighter by his sleeve and pointed. "There are people on the upper floor!"

Ryuu looked up. His gaze met Hiro's and his eyes went wide.

"Get a ladder up there!" Ryuu shouted. "Now!"

Two members of the fire brigade ran toward the building, carrying a bamboo ladder.

Hiro withdrew his head into the hall, which now was filled with thick, dark smoke and eerie orange light. Heat washed over him, scorching after the cold night air.

He stepped across the hall to the guest room door. "Come now. It's time to go."

A pair of quilt-covered figures appeared in the doorway in answer to his call.

Hiro grabbed Kintaro around the waist without removing the quilt from the child's head.

Kintaro screamed.

"Be still!" Hiro ordered.

Surprisingly, the boy obeyed.

Hiro thrust Kintaro's form through the window, hoping the fire brigade was there. To his relief, he felt strong arms relieve him of the burden.

"We have the child!" a male voice called.

Hiro stuck his head outside to see a firefighter moving down the ladder with Kintaro in his arms.

In the hallway, Father Mateo coughed.

Hiro turned to see the priest behind him, no longer covered with a quilt. Father Mateo clutched his Bible in one arm. In the other hand, he held the scabbard for Hiro's wakizashi.

Hiro took the scabbard from the priest and nodded to the window. "Go."

Father Mateo shook his head. "You—"

"GO!" Hiro thrust the scabbard through his obi, sheathed the wakizashi, and grabbed the Jesuit by the robe. "When the fire reaches the camphor paste in the hall, it will explode."

Father Mateo climbed awkwardly through the opening in the window, clutching his precious Bible in one hand. As the priest descended the bamboo ladder, Hiro swung his right leg through the window.

He blinked tears from his burning eyes as he tried to find the uppermost rung of the ladder with his foot. For a moment, it seemed to have disappeared. He thought the ladder might have fallen down.

"It's to your right!" Father Mateo called from the ground below.

Hiro shifted his foot and felt a surge of relief when his toes made contact with the upper rung. He swung his left leg through the window—and the camphor paste exploded in the hall.

The force of the blast blew Hiro off the ladder.

He flew backward through the air.

Below him, voices screamed.

Hiro felt his body falling toward the ground and turned his head to try and spot his landing.

As he did, his head struck something hard.

Bright stars exploded before his eyes, and the world went black.

CHAPTER 45

"H iro?"

He heard the voice, but could not remember where he was, or what had happened. His nose and throat felt burned. His ears were ringing. Fierce pain stabbed through his right knee. His head ached with a violence he hadn't felt in in many years.

In that instant, Hiro found himself transported back to Iga. He was lying face down in the snow, with Neko by his side. They had raided the sake brewery in the village the night before. He thought his head would burst from pain.

Beside him, Neko seemed to suffer no effects from the midnight binge.

He blinked, and found himself on the bloody floor of a steaming bathhouse, holding Neko's broken body in his arms.

His stomach lurched. He heaved.

"Roll him sideways!" someone shouted.

"No! Stop! He might be hurt!"

Hiro opened his eyes and shut them again immediately. The brilliant orange glow of the burning inn sent unimaginable pain through his aching head.

He rolled sideways just in time to vomit on the earthen street.

"Hiro," Father Mateo said. "Open your eyes."

I would rather not.

"Hiro." The Jesuit's voice was taut with fear. "Say something."

Hiro spat and used his hand to wipe the vomit from his chin. "Do you have a towel?"

He sensed Father Mateo move away and then return. A moment later, a wet towel wiped the shinobi's face.

Hiro forced his eyes open and reached for the towel. "Give me that." He closed his eyes again and rubbed the towel across his face. "What happened?"

"There was an explosion," the Jesuit said. "You fell."

"That, I remember." Hiro sat up slowly, ignoring the screams of protest from his head and knee. His left leg and his shoulder hurt as well, but seemed to be only bruised.

"Looks like you made it after all." Ana stepped into Hiro's line of vision, holding a bucket of water and several cloths. "Gato will be pleased."

"Gato's safe?" Hiro asked.

"Hm. Did you think I would leave her inside to burn? Of course she's safe."

Hiro smiled despite the pain.

A shout went up from the fire brigade as a line of men with hooks approached the inn. Columns of flame leaped from the upstairs window, sending sparks into the midnight sky. The blaze illuminated neighbors standing on the roofs of surrounding houses. Some poured water on the tiles, while others ran around with dampened towels, beating out any wayward sparks or cinders.

In the street, another crowd of neighbors threw buckets of water on the fire and the walls of nearby buildings, or chased down stray sparks and flames with dripping towels of their own.

"Matsui-*san*, I am so relieved to see you!" Kaeru approached him through the crowd.

She wore a winter kimono and a cloak. Her disheveled hair hung down her back, as if the fire had roused her from her bed, and she held a soot-stained towel in her hands.

She bent over him. "Thank the kami you escaped. I woke your servant, but the flames had already reached the stairs. I thought you perished."

"I'm sure you did." Hiro stood up slowly, gritting his teeth against the pain. His swords were gone, undoubtedly in the fall.

He reached up his sleeve, pretending to examine his wrist and arm as his fingers sought the hidden pocket inside his sleeve. To his dismay, he realized there was no pocket.

Why am I wearing someone else's clothes?

It took him several seconds to remember the river, Kintaro's rescue, and the bathhouse.

"I have no idea how the fire started." Kaeru looked at the burning building.

"You can stop watching," Hiro said. "He isn't coming out."

Kaeru's expression hardened, but by the time she turned around, she wore a look of innocent confusion. "I am afraid I don't know what you mean." She spoke a little louder than required, as if to ensure the crowd around them heard. "There wasn't anyone inside but you and the priest . . . and the boy, of course."

She shook her head. "I should have known better than to let the child spend the night, given his involvement in the other fires."

"It wasn't me!" Kintaro appeared at Father Mateo's side. He was holding Hiro's sheathed katana in his trembling hands. "You lit the fire! You tried to kill us all!"

"I have no time for a child's lies. I need to help the fire brigade." Kaeru walked away, angling toward the narrow space between the burning ryokan and the house next door.

Hiro took his sword from Kintaro.

Father Mateo laid a hand on Hiro's arm. "You're in no shape to fight."

"I cannot let her get away." Hiro's vision blurred. He blinked to clear it. "I have to do this, and I have to do it now."

"I'm coming with you—" the priest began.

"No. You need to stay and protect the boy. You heard her accusation. It's not safe to leave him here alone."

Before the Jesuit could argue, Hiro set his jaw and walked away.

CHAPTER 46

Kaeru paused for only a moment at the entrance to the walkway between the ryokan and the shop next door. The fire had not yet eaten through the outer wall of the inn, although it popped and crackled, warping the wood as the flames chewed through the structure like a beast devouring its cage.

"Don't go in there," a neighbor called. "It's far too dangerous. The flames will come through that wall at any moment. A group already left to go around the block and approach from the other side."

Instead of answering, Kaeru wrapped her dampened towel around her head and ran into the gap between the buildings.

A wave of heat, far stronger than the midday summer sun, struck Hiro's face as he approached the opening. The neighbor who warned Kaeru threw a bucket of water on the wall of the ryokan. The wood hissed as the droplets struck, its heat transforming them instantly into a cloud of steam.

"Don't go after her," the neighbor warned. "If the flames break through the wall, you'll burn to death."

Nausea rose in Hiro's throat. He felt unsteady on his feet. Only the pain in his knee and head allowed his thoughts to remain even somewhat clear.

He felt tempted to let Kaeru go.

It's not your mission. Let Hanzō hunt her down.

But if he made that choice, people would die . . . and Oda Nobunaga would get away with murdering more of the Iga ryu.

And that, Hiro would not allow.

He drew a breath in an unsuccessful attempt to calm his unruly stomach, gripped his katana, and hurried into the passage. Behind him, he heard the neighbors' shout of alarm, but he did not slow.

The air in the alley glowed orange. The air felt almost hot enough to burn.

Hiro held his breath and moved as quickly as he could. Near-blinding pain shot through his knee each time his right foot hit the ground. His eyes burned, and his throat and lungs felt raw.

Five seconds that seemed an eternity later, he reached the end of the passage and emerged into the common yard at the center of the block.

The temperature dropped sharply as he left the narrow passage, but his skin still glowed with remembered heat.

Neighbors stood on the roofs of buildings all around the open area, but the group that planned to fight the fire on the ground had not arrived. Fortunately, the flames had not reached the back of the ryokan either. Only the orange glow at the front of the building and the hazy, smoky air betrayed the fact that the building was on fire.

Kaeru waited several steps beyond the passage, watching the opening. When Hiro emerged into the yard, she turned away.

He drew a breath, paused long enough to ensure his voice was strong, and shouted, "Stop!"

She did, and slowly turned to face him.

He walked toward her, doing his best to hide his injuries.

When they stood face to face, she nodded to the sheathed katana in his hand. "You know you lack the strength to use that."

Hiro stared at her and did not answer.

"In a moment, I am going to turn around and leave," she said, "and you are going to let me do it. What happened here tonight will be our secret. Keep it, and you get to stay alive."

"The only way two people keep a secret is if one is in a grave," Hiro replied. "Ask Daisuke . . . and Natsu."

"I had such high hopes for that girl," Kaeru said. "I even arranged for her to marry one of Oda-*sama*'s highest-ranking samurai. She would have lived in luxury . . . but no. She chose a drug-confounded artisan. She deserved her fate."

"That's how you recognized Kintaro," Hiro said. "I thought you simply made a deduction, but you had seen his face before."

"From a distance only," Kaeru said. "Can you believe, Natsu was willing to become a mother to that brat? To turn her back on all her training . . . for a man?

"She hid the affair from me for months. She claimed she was working, but in truth she was sneaking out to meet him—I gave her everything, and she betrayed my trust!"

"That sword cuts in both directions," Hiro said. "Was the fire at Goro's shop your work as well, or merely the coincidence it seems?"

"That was a wasted opportunity." Kaeru shook her head in disgust. "Had I known the fool would set his own shop on fire, I would have had Daisuke eliminate Yasuari a week ago, and we would have avoided all this trouble."

Her tone grew soft, and more enticing. "If Hiroshi-*san* had married me, and not Midori, I would have ensured he became the leader of the Iga ryu when his brother died. It would be you, and not your cousin, in control of the clan right now. That part, at least, could still come true. Come with me. Join Daimyō Oda. When he claims the shogunate he will give you Iga—not just the ryu, but the entire province. You can rule it as your own."

"Daisuke made that offer too." Hiro blinked away another surge of dizziness. "My loyalty is not for sale."

Her expression twisted. "You are your mother's son."

"Thank you." Hiro forced a smile. "I consider that a compliment."

"It was not." She shifted her weight to the balls of her feet.

"Don't try to run," Hiro warned.

"I don't plan to."

Too late, Hiro saw the blade flash in her hand. He dodged, but felt the dagger bite his injured shoulder. He staggered sideways as he felt the blade strike bone.

He backed away and flung the scabbard off his sword. His right hand lacked the strength to wield the blade alone, so he gripped it with his left as well.

He barely raised the blade in time to block Kaeru's second strike.

He staggered two steps backward. She pressed the attack, staying too close for him to use the sword offensively.

He still could block, but he could not attack.

A second dagger appeared in her other hand. He had no time to wonder where it came from. She came toward him, stabbing high and low.

As Hiro tried to dodge, his knee gave way. He staggered sideways.

Kaeru lunged at him again.

Each time he deflected a strike, he struggled to pull the blade to a ready position fast enough to meet the next attack.

Shouts of alarm rang out from a nearby roof.

Hiro's vision swam and narrowed.

As he dodged another vicious blow aimed at his throat, he overcorrected. His knee buckled.

This time, he fell.

CHAPTER 47

As he dropped to the ground, Hiro tucked his head and rolled to the right, somersaulting away from Kaeru. He gasped as his injured shoulder struck the ground.

The earth spun wildly beneath him and then, somehow, righted itself again.

He rose to his knees as Kaeru swooped toward him, daggers raised to deal the killing blow.

Hiro had no time or strength to raise his blade for an upward strike. Instead, he swept the katana parallel to the ground. He felt the blade slice through Kaeru's kimono and her leg. He felt the distinctive pop as the sword severed the ligaments in her knee, and a jolt as the cutting edge struck bone.

Kaeru gasped, overbalanced, and crashed to the ground beside him.

Hiro forced himself to stand, but his right leg would bear no weight. He swayed, hopped once, and almost fell as a blinding flash of pain ripped through his head. Using only the toes of his right foot for balance, he managed to remain upright. He raised his sword.

Kaeru struggled to her feet as well. She had lost one dagger in the fall, but clutched the other firmly as she balanced on her own uninjured leg.

She stood with her back to the burning ryokan, silhouetted in the golden-orange glow of the flames that now appeared above the roof.

Dark streams of blood ran down her left calf and foot to puddle on the ground.

Behind her, the ryokan swayed.

Hiro blinked. When the structure moved again, he realized it was the firefighters, not his injured head, that made the building shift.

A shout rose from the far side of the building, followed by an enormous crash as the front half of the roof fell in.

The back door of the ryokan blew open, disgorging a gout of flame. A column of fire flew up from the burning roof. Embers swirled through the air like shooting stars.

"Surrender," Hiro told Kaeru. "You cannot run."

"Neither can you," she said.

"But they can." Hiro tipped his head toward to the people on the nearby roofs. His vision blurred, and another wave of nausea made him pause before continuing, "They saw you strike a samurai. One way or another, this ends for you tonight."

Kaeru laughed, but the sound contained no humor. "Any gambler knows the chance for gain carries an equal or greater risk of loss, especially when the stakes are high."

"This was never a game of chance," Hiro said.

"On the contrary." She made an expansive gesture. "This is all a game of chance. Sometimes you win. Sometimes you lose. If you're lucky, eventually you win big enough to escape the game before your debts come due. But if you lose, the debt comes due, and must be paid."

She dropped her dagger on the ground. "Tonight, I pay my debt in full."

Before Hiro could react, she turned, limped through the open door of the ryokan, and disappeared into the flames just as the back half of the ryokan collapsed around her.

A rush of heat blew outward, knocking Hiro off his feet. He tried to recover, but his right knee failed and he fell backward.

As he landed, his head bounced against the ground.

Black sparkles swam before his eyes, and darkness took him once again.

Hiro returned to consciousness as rough hands grasped his robe and pulled him across the rocky ground. The air grew cooler and the crackling sounds of the fire faded.

"Is he dead?" a male voice asked.

"Not yet." The answer came from somewhere very close. "But he needs help—"

Hiro groaned. To his relief, the unseen hands released him.

Footsteps moved away.

He sensed he was alone.

Hiro opened his eyes just enough to confirm that he was safe. He lay near the center of the communal yard, not far from the well. An ever-changing crowd of neighbors gathered there to fill their buckets and dampen soiled towels.

He hurt in so many places it was hard to evaluate which ones felt worst. He took inventory, moving downward from his throbbing head, but lost track halfway down and had to start again. To his relief, none of his injuries seemed life-threatening. The wound in his shoulder would take time to heal, but Kaeru's blade had struck his collarbone and glanced away, doing no lasting harm. He could not tell exactly what had happened to his knee, but did not think the fall from the window had broken any bones. His ears rang, and he knew the nausea would return if he moved too quickly, but that, too, should heal with time and rest.

Slowly, it occurred to him that Father Mateo probably wondered where he was, and what had happened.

Hiro closed his eyes. *I'll tell him later.*

He felt exhausted.

As he drifted toward unconsciousness, he tried to remember what his mother taught him about treating injuries to the head.

It will come to me after I get some sleep.

"Hiro!"

Father Mateo's panicked shout drew Hiro back from the brink of darkness.

He forced his eyes open and reached for his sword, only to realize he must have dropped it when he fell.

How many weapons will I lose tonight?

Footsteps pounded on the earth. Father Mateo knelt by Hiro's head. "What happened? Hiro, can you hear me?"

"Ahhh—don't shout." Hiro raised a hand and held his head. "Help me up."

The Jesuit hesitated. "Is that wise?"

"It's no more foolish than the other things I've done."

"Fair enough." Father Mateo slipped his hands under Hiro's shoulders and helped the shinobi to a seated position. "Where is Kaeru?"

Hiro started to nod toward the burning ryokan, but a surge of pain and nausea made him gesture with his hand instead.

"I don't see her . . ."

"She ran into the fire."

"Are you certain?" Father Mateo asked.

Hiro gestured to his face. "This happened afterward." Neither the comment nor the gesture made any sense—even to him—but the Jesuit merely nodded.

Hiro frowned. "It's cold. I need some water."

"What you need is a place to rest," Father Mateo said. "The man who owns the bathhouse on the corner offered to let us stay there tonight. I sent Kintaro back with him before I came to look for you. If you can get there . . ."

"I will get there." Hiro remembered his injured knee. "But I may need a little help."

CHAPTER 48

Hiro spent a painful night sitting upright against the paneled wall of a tiny room at the rear of the bathhouse. The space still smelled like the owner's ancient mother-in-law, and although Hiro appreciated the woman giving up her bedroom for their use, he felt less fondness for the musty, faded scents of cheap hair oil and dead chrysanthemums that lingered in the room.

Why do old women like those stinking flowers?

Hiro recognized his irritability as a byproduct of pain, the injury to his head, and lack of sleep, but indulged it anyway.

He shifted position restlessly.

In his lap, Gato woke up, stretched, and curled herself up again more tightly. Her rumbling purr rose in the silent room.

Just beyond his outstretched feet, Ana and Kintaro lay asleep on a pair of futons that almost filled the tiny room.

Father Mateo had insisted that the housekeeper and the child take the mattresses. He claimed he planned to stay awake all night and keep an eye on Hiro—who by then had come to his senses enough to remember that he should not sleep, at least for several hours. Now, the measured, even sound of the Jesuit's breathing—a perfect match to Ana's and Kintaro's—suggested that the night's events had caught up with the priest as well.

Hiro stroked Gato's fur as he reviewed and refined the story he would tell the magistrate at dawn. The facts constrained his tale more than usual, because the public explanation had to match Kintaro's version of events. His thoughts felt sluggish, but he persevered. By the time dawn's glow illuminated the slats of the narrow window, he had crafted a perfect narrative.

Nearly perfect, anyway, and it kept me awake as well.

With the task complete, and the immediate danger from his injuries past, Hiro rested his head against the wall, shut his eyes, and allowed himself to sleep.

He was briefly aware of movement in the room a while later, as Father Mateo and Ana woke Kintaro and silently left the room.

"Do you think it's safe to let him sleep?" the Jesuit whispered.

Hiro heard no response, but Ana's answer must have been affirmative, because they left him undisturbed. His stomach rumbled. He considered getting up to eat, but Gato's weight felt pleasant on his legs.

It wouldn't hurt to rest a little longer . . .

"Are you awake?" Father Mateo's voice, and the rumbling of the sliding door, brought Hiro back to awareness with a jump.

Gato stood up, stretched, and hopped off Hiro's legs. She wound around the Jesuit's ankles with a cheerful meow, requiring him to step around her as he walked into the room.

Bright sunshine streamed through the slatted window.

Hiro frowned. "What time is it?"

"Almost midday." Father Mateo smiled. "Ana checked on you every few minutes. She assured me it was safe to let you sleep."

Hiro stood up carefully. His knee protested, but it bore his weight. "We need to see the magistrate."

"I just returned from seeing him," the Jesuit said. "He asked me to convey his thanks, and that he hopes you make a fast recovery. Sora-*san* and Ishii-*san* send their regards as well. If you feel well enough—"

"Can I see him?" Kintaro stuck his head into the room. "Matsui-*san*? Are you alive?"

"Remember your manners!" Yuki appeared behind the boy.

She noticed the surprise on Hiro's face, and bowed to hide her smile. "I apologize for the intrusion, Matsui-*san*. Kintaro wished to thank you personally, as did I."

"I get to live with Yuki-*san*!" Kintaro's words bubbled out like a flowing stream. "She told the magistrate that I'm too young to be an apprentice, and he agreed. And since Ishii-*san* has to rebuild his shop, I can't work for him anyway. Yuki-*san* said I can live with her as long as I want to. And she even said that I can learn calligraphy." He turned to her. "Can I start today?"

"Perhaps tomorrow," Yuki said.

"You won't forget?" He gave her a worried look.

"If I do, I'm sure you will remind me." She bowed to Hiro once again. "Thank you for everything you've done. Kintaro and I will offer prayers at both the temple and the shrine for your safe travels."

"Thank you." Hiro barely avoided an instinctive nod. Although his head felt clearer, the dizziness had not abated.

"Now, please excuse us," Yuki said. "We do not wish to strain your strength. We merely wanted to convey our thanks."

"Do you really have to leave?" Kintaro asked. "Will you come back someday?"

"Kintaro." Yuki's voice held a warning tone.

"If God wills, perhaps we will return someday," Father Mateo said.

Kintaro nodded, though this answer clearly did not please him.

Yuki bowed again, and the two of them withdrew.

"What, precisely, did you tell the magistrate?" Hiro asked in Portuguese.

"The truth. Or an acceptable version of it, anyway. I told him Daisuke killed Yasuari during a dispute and set the fire at Ishii's shop to hide the body. As it turned out, Ryuu knew the location of Daisuke's storehouse—it belonged to the fire brigade, although only the commander had the key. The magistrate ordered the lock cut off, and we found a number of bloodstained baskets. At that point, it was easy to persuade the magistrate that Daisuke hid the murder weapon and the pot of camphor paste in Ishii's warehouse."

"How did you account for the fact that Ishii kept the warehouse locked?" Hiro asked. "Or did the magistrate not ask?"

"I told him Daisuke must have picked the lock to place the

evidence inside," Father Mateo said, "Hiyoshi was able to pick the lock on the day of the inspection, and you told me you can do it, so it seemed to make sense. The magistrate believed it, anyway."

"And the other fires?" Hiro asked.

"I saw no reason to disabuse him of the notion they were accidental."

"Including the one at the ryokan last night?"

"As it happens, Hiyoshi solved that problem for me. When I told the magistrate that we were sleeping when the fire began, Hiyoshi said that Daisuke most likely set that fire too, to prevent us from discovering the truth about his crimes, and that he must have fled from Edo to ensure that he would not be caught. Magistrate Hōjō found that answer reasonable, so I said no more."

After a pause, the Jesuit added, "I decided not to mention your fight with Kaeru, because I did not see it personally. One of the neighbors mentioned it to Hiyoshi, who told the magistrate, but I don't think the magistrate believed him."

"What did Hiyoshi say?"

"That she attacked you and then ran into the fire. After that, the hearing ended, and the magistrate appointed Hiyoshi to serve as the new head of the fire brigade." Father Mateo switched to Japanese. "Hiro, I owe you an apology. You were correct to suspect Daisuke. It was more than just a grudge."

"Perhaps, but your point was valid also," Hiro said. "I let my feelings blind me. Ultimately, the fact that my opinion was correct does not eliminate my error."

"I apologize anyway."

"And I accept it," Hiro said.

"Well, then," Father Mateo said. "Now that we've warned, or at least accounted for, all of the Iga agents on Hanzō's list . . . where do we go from here?"

Hiro had thought this issue through in the night as well. "Hanzō will expect us to head for the Portuguese colony at Yokoseura, where I can keep you safe until the emperor names a new shogun."

"I suppose, given your oath to the Iga ryu, we have no choice but to obey." Father Mateo paused. "Although, I also suppose there are multiple routes to Yokoseura . . . some more direct than others. For example, I've always wanted to travel through the mountains along the Kisoji. I hear it's lovely in the spring, though we may have to find a place to stay between here and there for a few more weeks, until the snow clears and the passes open."

Hiro raised an eyebrow at the priest. "If I didn't know better, I might think you were suggesting we ignore Hanzō's orders and strike out on our own."

"Hm." Ana appeared in the doorway. "That's precisely what he means, and you know it." She scooped the purring Gato into her arms. "What's more, I also want to see the cherry blossoms on the Kisoji."

"Then I suppose it's settled." Hiro smiled. "Yokoseura sounded boring anyway."

THE END

CAST OF CHARACTERS
(IN ALPHABETICAL ORDER)

Where present, Japanese characters' surnames precede their given names, in the Japanese style. Western surnames follow the characters' given names, in accordance with Western conventions.

Ana – Father Mateo's housekeeper

Daisuke – commander of the Edo fire brigade, and a member of the Iga ryu

Eiko – wife of Sora

Father Mateo Ávila de Santos – a Christian priest from Portugal

Gato – Hiro's cat

Goro – an artisan who carves the woodblocks used for making woodblock prints

Hattori Hanzō* – one of Japan's most famous ninja commanders, and leader of the Iga ryu; also known as "Devil Hanzō"

Hattori Hiro – a shinobi (ninja) assassin from the Iga ryu, hired by an anonymous benefactor to guard Father Mateo; at times, he uses the alias Matsui Hiro

Hiyoshi – a dōshin with the Edo police

Ishii – a bookbinder

Kaeru – an innkeeper and a member of the Iga ryu

Kenji – a calligrapher, and Kintaro's father

Kintaro – Ishii's apprentice

Magistrate Hōjō – the magistrate of Edo

Matsunaga Hisahide* – a samurai warlord who seized Kyoto in June 1565

Natsu – a member of the Iga ryu, posing as Kaeru's niece

Oda Nobunaga* – a samurai warlord who wanted to become the shogun and rule Japan

Ryuu – a commoner and a member of the Edo fire brigade
Sora – leader of the Edo bookmakers' and booksellers' association
(guild)
Susumu –a maker of woodblock prints
Yasuari – a member of the Iga ryu assigned to the Edo daimyō's per-
sonal guard
Yuki – Sora's sister

* Designates a character who, though fictionally represented, is based
upon a historical figure. [All other characters are entirely fictitious.]

GLOSSARY OF JAPANESE TERMS

D

daimyō: a samurai lord, usually the ruler of a province and/or the head
of a samurai clan

dango: bite-sized dumplings (often round) made from pounded rice
flour

dōshin: a low-ranking member of the medieval Japanese police; the
equivalent of a beat cop

F

futon: a thin padded mattress, small and pliable enough to be folded
and stored out of sight during the day

G

genkan: the traditional entry to a Japanese home or building

geta: traditional Japanese wooden sandals, consisting of a wooden base
elevated on two or three prongs

H

hakama: loose, pleated pants worn over kimono or beneath a tunic or
surcoat

harabuto mochi: a form of wagashi (traditional Japanese sweets) made
of mochi stuffed with various fillings

hojicha: roasted green tea, produced by drying and then roasting
green tea leaves, producing a rich, naturally sweet and nutty-
tasting tea.

hondo: literally, "main hall"; the building in a Buddhist temple where
the most important images and objects of worship are enshrined

I

itadakimasu: literally, "I humbly receive"; a traditional Japanese blessing or expression of thanks before a meal

J

jitte: a long wooden or metal nightstick with a forward-pointing hook at the top of the hand grip; carried by *dōshin* as both a weapon and a symbol of office

K

kami: the Japanese word for "god" or "divine spirit"; used to describe the deities of Japan's indigenous Shintō faith, the spirits inhabiting natural objects, and certain natural forces of divine origin
kanji: Chinese characters used for writing Japanese
katana: the longer of the two swords worn by a samurai (the shorter one is the wakizashi)
kimono: literally, "a thing to wear"; a full-length wraparound robe traditionally worn by Japanese people of all ages and genders
Kirishitan: the Japanese term for "Christian," specifically used to refer to the Roman Catholic priests who came to Japan during the 16th and 17th centuries
-kun: an affectionate diminutive, customarily used with children
kura: Japanese storehouses, typically built of wood, clay, or stone and used to store valuable items

M

miso: a traditional Japanese food paste made from fermented soybeans (or, sometimes, rice or barley)
mochi: glutinous rice, pounded to a uniformly smooth and chewy consistency

N

naginata: a Japanese pole weapon, similar to a halberd

netsuke: a miniature sculpture, usually 1–3 inches high, carved from bone, jade, or other materials; originally used as toggles to secure pouches and other items to the owner's sash

noren: a traditional Japanese doorway hanging, with a slit cut up the center to permit passage

O

obi: a wide sash wrapped around the waist to hold a kimono closed, worn by people of all ages and genders

onsen: volcanic hot spring bath

R

ronin: a masterless samurai

ryokan: traditional Japanese inn

ryu: literally, "school"; shinobi clans used this term as a combination identifier and association name (Hiro is a member of the Iga ryu)

S

sake (also "*saké*"): an alcoholic beverage made from fermented rice

sakura: cherry blossoms

-sama: a suffix used to show even higher respect than *-san*

samurai: a member of the medieval Japanese nobility, the warrior caste that formed the highest-ranking social class

-san: a suffix used to show respect

seiza: the traditional, formal way of kneeling or sitting in Japan

sencha: a variety of Japanese green tea

shinobi: literally, "shadowed person"; *shinobi* is the Japanese pronunciation of the word that many Westerners pronounce "ninja," which is based on a Chinese pronunciation of the written characters

shirazu: a pit of white sand, in which an accused person traditionally knelt to be judged by a magistrate in medieval Japan

shogun: the military dictator and commander who acted as de facto ruler of medieval Japan

shogunate: a name for the shogun's government and/or the compound where the shogun lived

shoji: a sliding door, usually consisting of a wooden frame with oiled paper panels

shuriken: an easily concealed, palm-sized weapon made of metal and often shaped like a cross or star, which shinobi used for throwing or as a handheld weapon in close combat

T

tabi: traditional Japanese socks, which have a separation between the big toe and the other toes, allowing them to be worn with sandals

tantō: a fixed-blade dagger with a single- or double-edged blade measuring six to twelve inches (15–30 cm) in length

tatami: a traditional Japanese mat-style floor covering made in standard sizes, with the length measuring exactly twice its width; tatami usually contained a straw core covered with grass or rushes

tokonoma: a decorative alcove or recessed space set into the wall of a Japanese room; a tokonoma typically holds a piece of art, a flower arrangement, or a hanging scroll, selected to reflect the current season

tsukemono: literally, "pickled things"; a general term for the pickled vegetables that typically accompany a traditional Japanese meal

W

wakizashi: the shorter of the two swords worn by a samurai (the longer one is the katana)

washi: traditional Japanese handmade paper

Z

za: guild

For additional cultural information, expanded definitions, and author's notes, please visit http://www.susanspann.com.

ACKNOWLEDGMENTS

It seems fitting that after eight books (and exactly a decade in "real-world time") Hiro, Father Mateo, and I have all ended up in Edo/Tokyo. However, while Hiro and Father Mateo got here on their own, I had an immense amount of help, for which I am exceptionally grateful.

Thank you, reader, for choosing to spend your valuable hours with Hiro, Father Mateo, and me. Your time is a gift, and I am grateful that my words received it.

Thanks to my agent, Sandra Bond, for almost a decade of hard work, dedication, and friendship. As I have said before, and will doubtless say again, you are the best friend and business partner any author could hope to have, and I am so glad we connected at Colorado Gold so many years ago.

Thanks to Dan Mayer, my talented editor, for giving Hiro and Father Mateo the chance to make this journey, and for making each novel stronger.

Thank you to Nicole Sommer-Lecht, for once again delivering breathtaking cover art. Your vision never fails to delight me.

To all of my friends in the United States and Japan: thank you for your constant help, support, and reinforcement. I could not do this—or anything else—without you.

To my son, Christopher: iron sharpens iron. Thank you for keeping my mental edges keen, my focus on the finish line, and my perspective in the proper place.

And, to the rest of my family: "thank you" is not enough—I love you all, so very much.

If you're still reading, thank you again for sticking around, and if you liked this book—or any other—please consider telling a friend.

Your praise, and your recommendation, are the greatest rewards an author can receive.

—Tokyo, Japan, January 2021